To Ea...

God B...

Kathi Harper Hill

Jeremiah 29:11

Falling

kathi harper hill

authorHOUSE®

AuthorHouse™
1663 Liberty Drive
Bloomington, IN 47403
www.authorhouse.com
Phone: 1-800-839-8640

First published by AuthorHouse 8/31/2009

ISBN: 978-1-4490-0761-4 (sc)

Printed in the United States of America
Bloomington, Indiana

This book is printed on acid-free paper.

To Anna Kate who informed me "Age is only a number."

Chapter One

*L*ela Sawyer stepped out of the hotel lobby and scooted carefully into the waiting cab. Despite her caution, the wires to the pain control unit hooked to her back tangled. Muttering under her breath, she tried to untangle them without pulling them from the machine, which was the only thing that kept her from unremitting pain. She blinked in surprise when she looked up to find a guy sliding in beside her. "Hey! What are you doing?" She asked indignantly. "This is my cab. Get your own!"

He slammed the door behind him. "Please let me stay! I'll pay the fare; I don't care where you're going. I just need to get off the street." He glanced nervously out the window. Careening around the corner were a half dozen teenage girls, looking frantically around. He hunkered down further in the seat.

Lela raised her eyebrows. "You're running from a bunch of thirteen year old girls?"

He grinned. "Yep. You'd think I'd get used to it."

"Okay," she said slowly. *Who was this guy?* The cab driver pulled away from the curb and was merged into the heavy traffic before Lela could protest further. "I guess you're going whether I want you to or not."

"Well, thanks anyway." Relieved, he continued. "I really will pay. I'm just grateful the cab was here and I have a fellow southerner to share the ride. Where're you from?"

She had also noticed *his* accent right away, somewhere in the back of her mind. "Georgia. You?"

He gave her a quizzical look and shrugged a little. "Same. A pleasant surprise to find a sister in the Big Apple. Have you moved here or just visiting?"

"Actually I'm headed to a hospital for a few days to have some tests run." She motioned toward the wires that disappeared up her back. "Nothing serious, just trying to find the solution that will fix me up. Do you live here?"

This time he *did* look at her oddly. She wasn't imagining it! "No. I'm here to – er – on business." He glanced down, almost as if he was embarrassed. He looked back up, a grin on his face. "I wouldn't live here for all the money in the world. I'm a true southerner to the bone."

She smiled. "So am I. This is the first time I've ever been to New York. And I hope the last." She started to speak again, but his cell phone rang, cutting her off.

"Sorry." He flipped it open, but before he could speak, she heard rapid-fire speech on the other end. Someone sounded none too happy. He closed his eyes and she saw his foot start tapping. She hid a smile. He didn't look too happy himself. "Look, I'm okay. I'm in a cab headed for-" His eyes popped open and he gave her an imploring look. She mouthed '*Saint Luke's*'- "Saint Luke's. No, I'm fine! I had to make a quick get away and I saw a cab with its door open. When I got in, I found it already occupied. That's where *she's* headed, I'm just ridin'". He grinned at Lela. "I promised her I'd pay the fare if she'd let me go with her." Whatever was said on the other end made him blush, which made the dusting of freckles across his nose stand out. He glanced at her, then away. "No, she doesn't know who I – I mean, I haven't introduced myself yet." He paused for more yammering from the phone. "Don't worry, I don't think she's overly impressed with me." He looked at her questioningly. She smirked. "Nope, she's not impressed at all. Huh? I don't know, how would I know that? Ha, ha. Very funny, Ted. No she's not a hundred years old." He looked at her again. "Are you?" She stuck her tongue out at him and he laughed. "I'm hangin' up. I'll turn this buggy around as soon as the lady gets out. I'll be back right away." Pause. Eye roll. "Yes, *Mother*." He snapped the phone shut, shaking his head. "Lord, I know that man means well, and I *pay* him well, but sometimes he is worse than my mama ever was!"

Thinking: *This guy must be someone really important,* she said, "Maybe he's just trying to do a good job."

"I know. But it gets old sometimes." He turned to her. "Does your job ever get old?"

"I haven't had a chance to find out. I was still in school working part time jobs when I had an accident. Since then I've had surgeries and rehab and only recently got my degree."

He looked embarrassed. "I'm sorry. I sounded ungrateful and I usually don't do that. I try to thank God for every day and every thing I have." Nodding toward the small unit clipped to her belt, he asked, "How long ago was your accident?"

"Almost two years ago. They can't seem to get things stabilized internally so that my pain is under control."

He looked as though a light bulb went off in his head. "So that explains it."

"Explains what?"

Startled, he asked, "Did I say that out loud?"

"Yes."

"Dang it! I have the worst habit of thinkin' out loud."

"Really? And what were you thinking, exactly?"

"Nothin' worth sayin'." The cab pulled into the hospital entry. "Let me help you with your bags."

"No, I just have the one. But thanks for offering. You really don't have to pay my fare. I don't think they'll charge extra for you." She smiled at him, her blue eyes bright.

"No way I won't. I said I'd pay it and I will." He stuck out his hand. "Thanks for saving me back there."

She laughed. "I don't think you were in too much danger."

He shook his head. "You have no idea."

She started into the hospital, still wondering who this guy was and why he obviously thought she should *know* who he was. She took a breath and turned around. "Wait – it was nice meeting you, but I never caught your name."

Once again that funny look crossed his face, then he smiled. She liked the way his eyes almost disappeared when he engaged his smile fully. "Henry. Henry Fields."

The name meant nothing to her. "Lela Sawyer. Nice meeting you Henry. Who knows? Since we're from the same state we might just meet again."

"I'd like that. I hope things go well for you."

"Thanks. Same to you." She walked in, the glass double doors closing slowly behind her.

He craned his neck and watched until he could see her shiny red hair no longer. He made sure the cabbie knew to return him to the hotel and sat back, smiling to himself. She really had no idea who he was! She had seemed to genuinely like him too. It had been getting harder and harder these past two years to know if anyone, especially females, liked him for him, or for what he did. He decided he'd be seeing Lela Sawyer again.

He flipped his phone up and punched a key. "Hey Ted. I want you to do me a favor. Yep, I'm on my way back. The girl that I rode with? Her name is Lela Sawyer, and she's being admitted to St. Luke's for tests. Find out what room she's in and stuff. I want to send her flowers. Maybe visit her." He listened for a minute. "Don't worry about that! She had no idea who I was. Nope, not a clue. Had some kind of accident a few years back and has had all kinds of surgeries and rehab. since then. I guess she's been out of the entertainment business loop." He listened again. "Well, you know I don't believe in luck. Meeting this girl was no fluke. God is always in control. Do you have any idea how nice it felt to be treated like an ordinary stranger? Everyone I've met the last two years acts like I'm either their best friend or a t-bone steak they want a bite of." The cab pulled up to the curb. "Hey, I'm here! No, I'll be fine, meet me in the lobby. Nobody is standin' out here anyway."

He dug in his pocket and handed the driver fare plus a generous tip. The cabbie grinned. "Thanks Hank. I recognized you immediately, but notice I know when to keep my yap shut."

4

Henry smiled back and gave the cabbie another twenty-dollar bill. "I appreciate it. Doin' that was worth more than a twenty, but that's all I got on me."

"You're welcome, son. The wife and I think you've got the best voice in the world, plus we admire the young man you are."

They shook hands and Henry exited the car. "Take care now." Henry watched the cabbie drive off, then he loped into the lobby, shaking his head slightly as he saw the giant bodyguard scowling at him. "Hey Ted. Cheer up. I didn't mean to escape. I'll be a good boy, I promise."

"Very funny, Hank. You can't just run off, not even for a second."

"All I really meant to do was step out and get a newspaper from the machine, but a bunch of girls saw me and started squealin'. *Which* alerted a photographer, *which* alerted a reporter, so I took off. I was gonna try and circle to the back, but I saw the open cab door and voila'! I disappeared right before their very eyes. You shoulda seen them lookin' for me."

Ted sighed. "It probably would have been better if you'd simply let them follow you back into the lobby. I was close by and so was John. Don't do that again, okay?"

Henry nodded. "I'm sorry. But let me tell you, sometimes I really do want to disappear, you know?"

Ted looked at him and softened. "I know, Hank. It has to be hard on you. But I'm here to take care of you. And some of your old buddies are flying in tonight to see the show, and they treat you like a regular guy, don't they?"

Henry agreed. "That they do. They wouldn't let me get away with anything."

Ted clapped Henry on the back. "Let's get you to your room so you can get ready. It's time to rock n roll, buddy."

Lela settled herself into the hospital room and sat down on the edge of the bed with a sigh. Her eyes welled up and she clutched the pillow to her chest. She'd never really been alone in her life and certainly not alone in a strange city, knowing absolutely no one. After the two

years she'd had and now in pain, all alone for tests, because her mother
had fallen so ill at the last moment her father couldn't leave her side!
She sighed again, shook her head and muttered, "Get hold of yourself.
You're a big girl and you're safe here." She bowed her head and said a
prayer of thanks for being kept under God's watchful eye.

As she prayed, she felt a tiny stab of guilt remembering the misleading
conversation about her "degree" with the guy in the cab. She'd worded
it to make herself sound older. But hey! A high school degree *was* a
degree, wasn't it? And a darned important one too! Besides, he was
cute and she knew realistically she'd probably never see him again. She
figured he was twenty-two or so, since he had a job already, and if he
thought she was that old too, that was fine with her. After all, she was
now officially an adult, if just barely.

She reached over and picked up the phone to call home. Her father
answered. "Hey Daddy. I'm checked in and safe. Is Mama getting
over the flu?"

"Lela! I'm so glad to hear from you. Your mother is much better,
and will be even more so as soon as she hears you're all right. Honey,
I'm so sorry you had to take this trip by yourself."

"Well, if they fix me up I'll be by myself pretty soon anyway, once
I start college."

"That's a bit different than traveling to New York City by yourself,
though. If someone had told me even last week I'd let you do this, I
would have laughed in their face!" He lowered his voice. "No one has
bothered you or anything have they?"

Henry Fields flashed through her mind. Mama would think the
story was cute, but her Daddy would see Henry as a big bad wolf, so
she'd save the story for her mother. "No one has bothered me, Daddy."
She said wearily. "The few people I've had contact with have been
extremely nice and helpful. You'll be glad to know almost all of them
have treated me like a child."

Her father chuckled. "Good. Let me hand the phone to your
mama. She's dying to hear your voice to make sure you really are fine.
I love you honey. Be very cautious."

"Yes, Daddy. I'll be careful. I love you too." She rolled her eyes
and waited for her mother to come on the line.

A whispery voice spoke. "Hey sweetie."

"Gosh, Mama, you sound awful! I thought Daddy said you were better!"

"I am, I am. This stuff has settled around my vocal cords and makes me sound worse than I feel. I am so relieved you're safe in the room. If you weren't in such pain we would have cancelled your trip till one of us could have gone with you. I feel so badly about this!"

"It's fine, Mama, really. When I'm discharged, I'll go straight from here to the airport and then I'll be home. It's not like I'm on the streets or anything."

"How are you feeling? Don't forget to tell the doctor about your abdominal pain."

"I'm doing all right. And I won't forget to let them know the surgeon said the pain is really coming from my back."

"Good girl. Was the hotel nice last night?"

"Yes. And the cab pulled up right outside the door and brought me directly here."

"So no uneventful episodes, huh?"

Lela giggled. "Well, there was one funny thing, except I didn't think Daddy would laugh, so I saved the story for you."

Her mother had been a little amused, but more alarmed than Lela would have guessed. So Lela left out the fact that she and Henry had exchanged names. No point in making her mother worry, especially with her sick and all.

She was saved from the second nudge of conviction because she had no sooner hung up than there was a knock on the door. A giant bouquet of multi-colored flowers hid the woman bringing them in. "Hello there! You must have a wonderful boyfriend!" The lady chirped, snapping her gum. She plopped the vase down on the widow sill. "Will this spot do?"

"That's fine." Lela said. "Who in the world could they be from?"

"There's a card. It's a guy." She pulled the card off the holder and handed it to Lela. "Hope your stay is a good one." She winked and turned to go.

Lela opened the envelope and flushed pink. She glanced up at the lady as she was leaving. "Thank you." She called to the retreating back. The woman gave a backward wave and was out the door.

The flowers were from Henry! The card read: *'Thanks for not throwing me to the curb! Henry'.* Lela smiled. She'd never received flowers from a boy before. She reached over and slipped the card into her purse for safekeeping, then spent a few moments wishing she was at home and he was a local and they could start seeing each other, and…well, on and on. She finally scolded herself and turned on the television. She was *not* going to start mooning over missing her last years of high school, boyfriends, prom, sports or anything else. What had happened, had happened, and she couldn't change the past.

Finally, after a fairly decent supper tray, a little television, and a last check by the nurses, she'd tucked herself in, felt terribly homesick, said a quick prayer and fallen asleep.

Lela opened her eyes to sunlight. After a fitful night's sleep, she was startled to find Henry sitting in the chair by her bed, dozing. She grinned. He looked all of twelve years old with his face relaxed and free of expression. His curly blond hair was in wild disarray, and far too long. She felt a pang of envy looking at those gorgeous eyelashes that lay on his cheeks like a fan. *Why do guys get the long lashes, when it's girls who want them so badly?* She thought to herself. Aloud, she said, "Hey sleepyhead, what are you doing here?"

He opened one green eye, squinting at her. "Hey yourself. I was tryin' to sleep. I came all ready to visit and you were snorin' like a lumberjack."

"I'll have you know I don't snore! I think. Do I really?" she felt her face grow warm.

"Nah. But you *were* asleep. I was tired anyway, and I thought I'd take advantage of the moment." He yawned and stretched. She thought he looked about ten feet tall.

"I'm surprised to see you. But I think I was more surprised by the flowers." She nodded toward the wildflowers that adorned the windowsill. "Trying to score a date for the prom?"

Henry gave a short laugh. "Oh, yeah. You've got my number, you're so on to me." He stood up and came over to her side. "I'm usually not a very pushy person, but I didn't know how to contact you if I waited till you were discharged." He smiled slightly. "I really enjoyed our little ride together and I wondered if you would like to go to dinner or something when we both get back home."

"Well, I guess that'd be okay Henry, if we even live close enough to one another to go out to dinner."

"I can come to where ever you are."

Lela was surprised. "Oh really? That might get expensive. And what about your job?"

"Let's just say my job is very flexible. And let's also say my job pays well enough that money ain't a problem."

Lela tilted her head and looked at him intently. "Okay." She thought a moment. "Are you trying to tell me your parents are rich?"

Henry laughed again. "Hardly. My folks are great people but fortunately for all concerned I don't have to depend on them financially anymore." He looked like he was about to say more, then changed his mind. "What about you? Are you a little rich girl?"

"Not at all. My parents are both in the helping profession. Daddy teaches special education and Mama works with families who have kids suffering from emotional problems. We have always lived comfortably, but with those kind of careers you'll never see rich."

Henry's face lit up. "I was gonna be a teacher too!"

"What happened?"

"Well, I, um, got sidetracked." Lela could tell he was struggling about telling her something, and it was clear to her she had *missed* something that he thought obvious to everyone. He looked up at her. "Do you believe God has a plan for your life and sometimes it's not the same plan you have for yourself?"

"Duh. Look at me. I've been raised to believe that there are no coincidences or fate. So I have this terrible accident that totally changed my life. If I didn't believe God knew what He was doing, I don't think I could have any faith at all." Tears filled her eyes.

Henry softened and he found himself reaching up to touch her face. "In that case, I expect you believe I didn't fall into that cab by accident either. I certainly don't. I was telling Ted last night that meeting you was no coincidence and I wanted to talk to you again." He stuck his hands in his pockets and turned from her. "The last year or two of my life has been very different too, Lela. My whole life has changed, turned upside down. I've had to be careful with who I trust and make friends, what to say, where to go… it's just been hard." He turned back around to her. "Not hard like your life. But hard, nevertheless." He plowed through his hair with both hands. "When do you blow this joint?"

Lela grinned at him. "Unless I can escape earlier, it will be tomorrow. Then I catch a flight to Atlanta."

"Is that where you live?"

"No, I live further north, up in the mountains. My parents will pick me up at the airport and take me home."

"If I can arrange my schedule, maybe we could fly out together."

Lela hesitated. "Henry, I don't know - I mean-"

"You're right." He stopped her with a shake of his head. "What was I thinking? Then he grinned at her. "It's just a plane ride, Lela. But maybe there's some way I could prove to you I'm above board."

"I didn't mean I don't think you're safe…I - well, I don't know exactly what I did mean, but-"

"Look, I understand. I mean, how would you know more than I'm a guy who kidnapped your cab? Let's see," Trying not to laugh, he said, "I know! I'll have my mama call you. No, wait, how would you know she's my mama? Okay, okay, how about Ted? No, you don't know Ted either…"

Lela began to giggle. "Stop! I don't know how anyone could think you're anything more than a goober! All right, we'll fly out together if you can swing it." She glanced downward. "I guess I'm a little uncomfortable because we don't know each other. I'm a little stunned by all the attention." Embarrassed, she peeked at him from under her eyelashes.

"Yeah, and how else can we get to know each other, unless we spend time together? I like you enough already to want to know you better. And I am way more than a goober, thank you."

"No way."

"Way."

As they were grinning foolishly at each other, the door swung open and a smiling young nurse walked in. "Lela, it's time to take your-," She glanced up and the smile froze on her face. She dropped the medications and screamed. "Ohmygoodness! Do you know who you are?!"

Lela looked as dumbfounded as Henry looked embarrassed. Lela glanced over to him, as if for protection from this crazed nurse. "Yes, I know who I am." He smiled at the nurse, adding a pleading look to it, which did no good at all.

"Oh, I just can't believe it! Hank Fields! Right here! I can't believe it!" She seemed to come to herself a little. "Oh, look at me, you must think I'm an idiot! I've dropped meds everywhere." She bent to scoop up the two capsules that had rolled from the pill cup. "I'll be right back with more." She swung on Henry. "And don't you dare move! Don't go anywhere, I've *got* to have your autograph!" She walked out the door and then came back in immediately. "And don't worry, I swear, I won't tell a soul. Don't move!" And without waiting for a reply she fled the room.

Lela turned to Henry. "What the heck was that all about?"

Henry blushed. "Have I mentioned I might be, um, a little, uh, famous?"

"Famous?! I knew something was up with who you are, but no, you haven't mentioned anything like that ! "

The nurse chose that moment to re-enter. She shoved the pill cup toward Lela, never taking her eyes off Henry. "Here. Take this." She reached over to pour Lela water, looking over at Henry the whole time. "Gosh, you're even cuter up close. And so tall!" She turned back to Lela. "Drink the whole glass full so the pills will dissolve." Back to Henry, "Are you singing at "*The Hall*" again tonight?"

"Yes, at seven. Do you have tickets?"

Her face fell. "No. I don't get off till seven anyway. But I saw you last spring. Twice! I am *so* like your biggest fan! I have both your CD's too." She stuck her hand in her pocket and came out with a scrap of paper. "Can I have your autograph?"

"Sure." He scribbled his name and handed it back to her. "But please," He glanced at her nametag, "Beth, please don't tell anyone I'm here. You can share after Lela's discharged. Will you wait as a favor to me?"

"Oh, how did you know my name?" She gave a little squeal and looked happily at Lela. Lela slowly pointed to Beth's nametag. "Oh, of course, how stupid of me! I feel so dumb!" She smiled at Henry. "Of course I won't tell anyone till you're gone. Hey, I'd probably get fired if I caused such a ruckus!" She took a deep breath. "So, is Lela your baby sister or something?"

Lela felt her hackles rise. *Baby sister!* But Henry came to the rescue. "No, actually Lela is a good friend. I'm trying to keep her company till we can go back home."

Beth's face fell again. "Oh. Well." She turned and smiled down at Lela. "You are one lucky little chick. To have a *'friend'* like Hank, I mean." She looked at Henry and smiled bigger. "It was *so* nice meeting you! Thank you *so* much!" she gushed and floated from the room.

Lela rolled her eyes. "And she is *so* over the top! What are you, a rock star?"

Henry looked at the floor. "As a matter of fact, I am."

"Yeah, right, I - wait." Lela looked at him closely. "Are you serious?"

He sighed. "Yeah, for a couple of years now. The timing is why you didn't know."

"Why, for the love of pete, didn't you tell me?!" Lela, narrowing her eyes, pushed herself up straighter in bed. "I feel like a fool!"

Henry sat up straighter too. "What was I supposed to do? Hi, I'm Hank Fields, rock star? It finally dawned on me you didn't have a clue who I was, and I didn't know how to tell you; and frankly, I liked knowing that you might actually be enjoying my company thinking I was just a –a – goober!" he finished triumphantly.

Was God playing a joke? A *rock* star? Lela fell back on to the bed, the wind going out of her sails. "I don't know what to say. I guess I won't have to do much to check you out, huh?"

"Shouldn't be too hard. Of course, depending on what rag you read as to what you'll find out about me. I've been accused of everything but ax murder. That's probably in '*The Star*' next week." He added glumly. "If you want to know what kind of guy I am, ask people who know me. Really do ask Ted. He works for me, but he's a friend too." Henry stood up and ran his hand through his hair. "I hate the way this happened. I was gonna try and tell you over a nice dinner and invite you to a show when you felt up to it. I'd still like to do that, if you're willing to give me a chance."

Lela thought for a moment. "It sounds like fun. I have to get used to this, though. I really did think you were just a goober."

"Well, don't tell anybody, but I'm afraid you are absolutely correct." Henry whispered softly.

Chapter Two

*H*enry left the hospital relieved Lela hadn't freaked out when she found he was famous and even more relieved that she hadn't treated him any differently afterwards. Maybe there actually was someone on the planet who didn't care about his fame.

Upon his return to the hotel, he hurried to his room and made flight arrangements. Then he flopped onto the bed, kicked off his sneakers, and called his father. Henry told him about Lela.

His father listened patiently, then asked, "So you're going to fly with this girl you stole a cab from and then what?"

"I don't know, Dad. But at least she doesn't have ulterior motives. It's the first time I've felt that way for a while about anybody new in my life." Henry stood and paced. "I want you and Mama to pray about this. She seems like a sweet girl. I'll meet her daddy and maybe her mama at the airport. I thought I'd ask them to lunch, or something."

"Whoa, son! Are you going to ask her daddy for her hand while you're at it?"

'Here we go.' Henry thought. Aloud, he said, "No, of course not. You just don't understand. I have to be back on the road and I need to at least be with her a little to see if I want to pursue getting to know her."

"I do understand, Henry. I may understand better than you. You're young and you've been thrown onto a lonely road. You have to be hyper-vigilant all the time so you're not taken advantage of or mobbed. You want to let down your guard for a change, and I don't blame you. Still, you have to be careful, not only for your sake, but for hers. You don't want to hurt her."

"I promise I'll be careful. Will ya'll pray?"

"You're in our constant prayers, Henry. We will be very precise about this." His father paused for a moment. "We miss you, son. I see you on T. V. more than I do in the flesh. I'm glad that you get to come home for a visit. Is Ted bringing you from the airport, or do I need to pick you up?"

"Ted will bring me to the house. Then he can have my car and I'll use yours or Mama's if that's okay. He is as homesick as I am and I figure it won't hurt to let him get home as soon as he can."

"Sounds good. We'll see you then. Take care, Henry. We love you."

"I love you too, Daddy. Tell Mama the same. Bye." Henry sat on the edge of the bed and looked heavenward. "Lord, are parents *supposed* to try and make you feel stupid?" He shook his head. He wasn't trying to take advantage of Lela, just get to know her, and what was wrong with that?

Lela grew nervous as she waited in her hospital room for Henry. She'd talked to her parents the night before with full intentions to tell them about Henry, but she hadn't. When it came right down to it, what was there to tell? She was riding on the same plane with him, but so what? She was a small town girl just trying to get her life back and Henry was, well, *famous,* whatever else he might have been or be now. How could that mean much for them, other than maybe an occasional phone call? She hadn't studied up on the life of the rich and famous, but she didn't have to in order to know it was nothing like her own.

A quick knock on the door brought her back to the present. Henry peeked in. "Your chariot awaits you, madam." He was pushing a wheelchair. "They said you have to ride in this to the car. I've got a limo waiting on us."

"Well *that* ought to keep us from getting a lot of attention."

"Hey, I wanted you to ride in style." He shrugged. "Even though I can afford it, I never actually use one, 'cause you're right. It draws attention, and that's usually the last thing I want." He winked at her. "Unless, of course, I'm on stage." He picked up her bag and the vase of flowers as a nurse came in to assist Lela into to the wheelchair to prevent tangling up her wires. Lela reached for her purse and sat it in her lap. She cruised the room with her eyes, making sure she was forgetting nothing. "Ready?" Henry asked. "Let's get outta here."

Lela glanced at the vase of beautiful wildflowers Henry held. "Would you mind if we gave these to a patient who needs cheering up?" She blushed a little. "They did that for me."

"That's a great idea, Lela." Henry replied. "Hold on." He handed the vase to the nurse, broke one of the bright pink lilies off and handed it to Lela. "That's to remember me by." He turned back to the nurse. "Will you see they go to someone special?"

The nurse smiled and promised she knew just the patient who would be cheered by them. As they passed the nurse's station, she handed the flowers off, giving instructions to the pink lady.

Lela got lots of grins and waves as Henry rolled her down the hall. The accompanying nurse was obviously impressed by the sleek, black limousine awaiting them. Flustered, Lela tangled up the wires attached to the unit on her back. It took the nurse and Henry to get them straightened out and plugged back up. Lela turned bright red when Henry held her shirt up a little in the back for the nurse to re-attach the wires. Seeing that she was embarrassed, Henry didn't tease her, as was his nature. He hoped he'd soon have a chance to learn when it was safe to tease.

Lela began to feel less conspicuous as the sleek automobile sailed anonymously down the freeway. She settled back in the soft leather seat. "So tell me how in the world you wound up in the music business."

Henry thought for a moment. "Well, I think I told you I was planning on a teaching career?" Lela nodded. "My cousin asked me to sing at his wedding. A few days later his bride to be called and asked if I could get a band together and sing at the reception too. I did, and during break a guy came up to me saying how impressed he was with my voice, and wondered if I had ever thought about recording a CD.

I told him I had done a demo for my folks and friends and he sort of looked funny at me and said no, no, he meant a *real* CD. He asked me would I consider it if he could get some backing." Henry laughed. "So what was I supposed to say – no? Of course I said yeah, sure, not really believing I'd hear from him again." Henry took a deep breath. "So imagine my surprise when two days later I got a call from him. He sounded odd at first and I thought he was going to politely back out. Instead he said my cousin had let him borrow the video from the reception for his "friend in the business" to see. They had watched the tape and wanted me to be a guest on *"Happening New York"* the following week. I nearly fell out of my chair! The next thing I know I'm recording a CD, I'm on all the talk and entertainment shows *and* I'm doing a tour. Wham! My whole life changed."

Lela shook her head in wonder. "Well, my goodness. See what you miss when you fall down?"

Henry smiled at her. "I wish you hadn't fallen down, but I am glad you missed the hoopla. Sometimes I wish *I'd* of missed it." He tilted his head looking at the wires creeping up her back. "How did you get hurt, anyway?"

"Clumsiness. I went on a ski trip, and like I said, I fell down. I broke eight bones and I've had three surgeries, including one to regulate my heartbeat, who knows what *that* was about."

"So, were you skiing down a big mountain?"

Lela looked embarrassed. "No, I was walking on a level sidewalk. They'd cleared it of snow, but then there had been a little sprinkle of rain and it froze. This formed what they call 'black ice' because you can't see it. I didn't even notice the walk looked wet. They tell me I slid right onto the street into the path of an oncoming car. When the car hit me, I sailed about twenty feet into the air before landing. I don't remember any of it though."

"I'd say that's more than just falling down! Are you ever gonna be free of pain?"

"I don't know. I keep thinking time is on my side. The doctors say I'm young and I should be fine, but it's taking me so long to heal. My pain receptors have gone haywire. I never know when I'm going to wake up in the middle of the night in terrible pain. Which is ridiculous! They don't even know why. I just hope this set of tests can give us some answers." She looked up at him and smiled a little. "Are you sure you want to be buds with a wimp?"

He reached down and touched her cheek. "Yeah, I'm pretty sure. Are you sure you want to be buds with a goober?"

"Yeah, I'm pretty sure."

"Do you think your parents will like me?" Henry asked, feeling suddenly nervous.

"What's for them not to like, Henry? For all I know, they're in the loop and have heard of you, unlike their dorky daughter."

"Somehow that doesn't make me feel any better. I know *my* folks would love *you*. They'd see you as potential." Henry waggled his eyebrows at her. "They already talk about how am I ever gonna meet anyone and settle down, cause who can you trust? And I never really fell for anybody before fame. Even though I've got lots of friends, that's just what they are. Friends."

"Maybe things won't always be so crazy for you and you'll have a shot at normalcy as time goes by."

"You know how parents are. If there isn't something to worry about they'll make something up."

"Yeah. My parents are pretty protective, maybe because I'm an only child. But oddly enough this accident has allowed me to grow up a little bit. Like traveling to New York alone. Of course, that wouldn't have happened if Mama hadn't got sick at the last minute. But I'm an adult, and it wasn't like I was going all over the place once I got there. They didn't like it, but they let me."

"Let you? I guess once you're an adult they have to, huh?"

Lela squirmed a little in her seat. "Well, yeah, but I think me getting hurt made them feel like I was helpless, and I was, at least at first."

Henry glanced up as the limo slowed. "We're here. I changed your ticket to first class so we can sit together." He looked at her shyly. "Would you like to listen to some of my music on the plane ride?"

"Oh, Henry, I'd love to! I was wondering last night how quickly I could buy a CD and catch up." She grabbed his arm and looked at him, unsmiling. "What if I don't like it?"

Henry blinked. "I hadn't thought of that. I guess just tell me."

Lela grinned. "I'm kidding. I'm sure I'll love your voice."

"I stay on key, you can understand what I'm singin' and I don't use foul language. Other than that, you'll have to decide for yourself. And I'm fragile, don't *ever* tease me again!"

Laughing, Henry helped Lela get out of the limo as the driver retrieved their bags. They boarded the plane and were soon airborne.

Lela had not seen Ted, Henry's bodyguard, on the plane, but he quickly materialized and met them upon disembarking. After formally meeting Lela and assisting them in retrieving baggage, he stayed a respectable distance away from parental introductions until Henry called him over.

Henry insisted on taking them all out to lunch upon leaving the airport. Lela's parents *had* heard of "the famous Hank Fields", but admitted they wouldn't have recognized him.

The restaurant was small, dark and expensive. Ted requested a table in the back. Their lunch was interrupted only once by an over eager teeny bopper, but she was polite and almost ran away from their table as soon as she got Henry's autograph. Grinning at the retreating teen's back, Lela shared the story of the star struck nurse at the hospital.

Lela's father, Art, turned to Henry. "Does this kind of thing happen everywhere you go?"

Henry shifted in his seat. "Yes sir, I'm afraid it does. That's why Ted goes with me when I travel. I never know when an overly enthusiastic person will turn into a crowd. I've been hurt a couple of times." He shook his head and grinned. "By girls."

"Ouch." Art sympathized. "Flattering and embarrassing at the same time." He turned to Ted. "Have you been in this business for long?"

"When I was younger I was body guard to and toured with the worst of them. It got old quick, so I started working gigs strictly around Atlanta, so I could be home with my family. Then Hank came along." Ted shrugged. "He's my job most of the time right now. My wife and I care about him like he's our own."

Vicki, Lela's mother, spoke up. "Well, Henry, I guess Ted's presence comforts your parents a great deal."

"Yes ma'am. I don't think they'd like the preacher at my funeral telling their friends I was trampled by a bunch of thirteen year olds."

Lela snickered into her napkin, trying to pretend it was a cough. The rest of them looked at her and then burst out laughing. Henry affected a reproachful look. "I can see the abuse will continue from the female population, no matter how much protection I have."

After a pleasant meal, Henry and Lela hugged each other good-bye. He insisted she have his private cell phone number. She gave him the same in return and then impulsively kissed him on the cheek before leaving him.

In the two weeks since, Lela heard from Henry every day. During one of their conversations Lela discussed tests results from her doctor visit. "They found a pinched nerve causing some of the pain. They insist that's where the abdominal pain is from, too. The doctor suggested a nerve block to see if that will help. They changed some of my medications and tell me time will have to pass before any level of success can be measured."

"When are you havin' the nerve block done?"

"Tomorrow. I'm dreading it. I guess I'm scared. The nurse said it's a safe thing, but I've had so much done," Lela paused as her voice got shaky.

"I've been prayin' for you, Lela. It's gonna be alright." Henry's voice softened. "God's seen you this far, He won't abandon you."

"I just feel sorry for myself sometimes."

"We all do that." Henry took a deep breath. "Well, this will either cheer you up or make you feel worse."

"What?" She asked cautiously.

"The tour is over next week and I am officially off work for a while. What do you say to askin' your parents if I could visit for a few days?"

"Henry, that sounds like fun! Of course I'll ask."

"We've got a couple of hours in rehearsal, but no show tonight, so I should be free after nine thirty or so."

"Well, then, you call me when you're finished."

"There's some exciting news I want to share with you."

"Yeah, what?"

"Ain't sayin'. Gotta keep some mystery about myself, you know."

"I thought it was the women who were supposed to be mysterious."

"When you look as dorky as I do, you have to have some kind of gimmick to keep the girls interested."

"*Girls?* Plural?"

"Girl! I mean girl!"

"That's better. Call *this* girl tonight, buster."

Lela was shocked at her parent's enthusiasm. Her mother ordered Lela to find out what Henry's favorite foods were and did he sleep warm or cool? That question embarrassed Lela to no end, but she'd asked and Henry laughed at her obvious discomfort. He said, "I eat anything Southern and in the winter I like my bedroom cold. That comes from not having central heat when I was a little kid so my bedroom wasn't warm. Now *I* have questions. What kind of perfume does your mama wear and what kind of gadget does your daddy not have?"

With one last phone call, she gave him suggestions for gifts (reminding him she wanted a present too), and let him know the nerve block was done with results that pleased the doctors.

Henry teased her about wanting a present. "Maybe I'll get you two presents. Earrings would be two presents, right?"

"Oh, you are *such* a goober." She sighed. "I really am looking forward to seeing you, in spite of you gooberishness. I can't believe how much I have missed you." She felt herself turning red and thought '*how could I have said that?*'

There was a moment of silence "Really, Lela? I've missed you too. I was afraid it was just me. I mean, we haven't known each other long, but every time we talk I feel so connected to you. I haven't said much 'cause I didn't want you to think I was pushy or make you feel uncomfortable."

"I feel fine. And we have plenty of time, right?"

"All the time in the world. And you have made me look very forward to it." Afterwards, Lela hugged the phone to her chest for a moment, said a prayer for them both and felt so happy she thought she'd burst.

Lela paced her bedroom until she was sure the pale pink carpet was paler in spots. She badly needed to talk to someone about all this. She knew she could trust Emmie; they had been friends since church nursery when they took turns drinking from the same baby bottle. She was a good friend. Lela finally picked up the phone.

After they chatted aimlessly for a while, Lela said, "I've got something to tell you."

"Okay, shoot. What is it?" Lela could almost see Emmie lounging by the pool, twirling one lock of dark auburn hair around her finger, brown eyes half closed against the sun.

"I met someone while I was in New York."

"You mean like a guy?" Emmie's voice perked up.

"No, I mean exactly a guy."

"Very funny. Is he a doctor or was he a patient?"

"Neither. And guess what? He lives in Georgia. About two hours from here."

"How weird is that? Well, we know God works in mysterious ways, huh? Have you talked to him since?"

"Just every day. And he's coming up to visit."

"How do your parents feel about that?"

"They like him. He had the same flight home as I did and we all ate together after we landed in Atlanta."

"Lela Sawyer, why haven't you told me this before? What's this guys name?"

"His name is Henry. I haven't told you before because it's a little complicated."

"I'm coming over. Can I come right now?" Emmie sounded like she was already getting her keys.

Lela laughed. "Sure. In fact, I was hoping you'd say that. I really need to talk, Emmie. I'll fix a snack and we can chat in my room."

"You bet. I'll be there in half an hour."

Emmie was true to her word, and they settled into Lela's room. Henry's CD case was lying on the bed, and Emmie picked it up. "You like Hank Fields, huh?"

Lela, startled, turned around to stare at Emmie. "How did you know?"

"Well, I don't. But I see you bought the CD, so I'm asking: do you like it or not?"

"Oh." Lela flushed. Emmie quirked an eyebrow. "Yeah. I love it. I've been out of the music loop for a while, so I was surprised how much I'd missed music as I listened to it. It's a great CD. Have you heard it?"

"I've heard the single they released to radio. I like it pretty good. I'm thinking about buying the CD." Emmie turned the case over. "He's kinda cute, you know? In a dorky sort of way. I mean, he's got a nice smile." Before Lela could respond, Emmie continued. "Of course, I don't know how nice he *is*. I saw in a magazine where he was coming out of some bar or something and his eyes looked like he was about three sheets to the wind."

"He doesn't drink."

"Where'd you read that?"

"I didn't read it." Lela sat on the bed, looking up at Emmie. "I'm guessing you saw that in a tabloid, right?"

"Yeah. I was reading it while I waited in line at the store. The article said he'd refused an interview and had been totally rude to them."

"I bet. Look, Emmie, you shouldn't be reading that junk, you know it's full of made up stuff. And besides, we aren't supposed to gossip about people. Christ hates that kind of stuff."

Emmie's eyebrows shot up. "I'm not gossiping. Well, not exactly. It's not like I know the guy, he's a celebrity. What I say's not going to hurt his feelings, he'll never know. Plus, being famous, they ask for it."

"Oh, really? How did he ask for some piece of garbage to make stuff up about him?"

"Gosh, Lela, calm down. It's just a stupid tabloid story about some singer. It's no big deal." She tossed the CD case to the foot of the bed and sat down next to Lela. "Now, tell me about Henry. That's what I really want to hear."

"That *is* Henry."

"What *is* Henry?"

"That's who we've been talking about. Henry."

Emmie looked at her, a blank stare on her face. "We've been talking about tabloid gossip and what a bad person I am to read it."

"And how bad they are to say stuff about people like Henry that isn't true."

"Huh? Lela, we've been talking about Hank Fields. You know, pop star? Not Henry – what's his last name?"

"Fields."

"Fields. Fields? Henry Fields? *Hank Fields* is your new boyfriend?" As Emmie finished the sentence her voice got higher.

"Yeah. Hank Fields is my friend."

Emmie squealed. "I can't believe this!" She squealed again. Then she grabbed the CD case, clutched it to her, and really squealed. "How on earth did you meet him?"

"We shared a cab in New York and then he sent me flowers and visited me in the hospital. He arranged to be on the same flight back to Atlanta so we could sit together. We've been talking ever since. And now he's coming to see me."

Emmie sat, stunned. "I can't believe it. Wow. No wonder you got so ticked about the tabloid thing." She turned to Lela. "You know people don't believe that stuff anyway."

"No? Then why were you repeating it like it was the gospel?"

Emmie blushed. "You're right. I'm sorry. Wait a minute and I'll take my foot out of my mouth." She smiled weakly at Lela. "Forgive me?"

Lela sighed. "Yes. This just isn't going like I planned. I'd hoped we'd be all happy and instead I'm half mad at you."

"I truly am sorry, Lela. You know me; I learn my lessons the hard way. I promise I won't read or talk about junk journalism anymore. And if I hear anyone else doing it, I'll knock 'em up side of the head, how's that?"

Lela smiled a little. "Sounds good." They hugged. "Now, Emmie, you have to promise me you won't share what you know with anyone. Henry and I hardly know one another and I don't want him followed up here by a bunch of fans or photographers."

"Sure. When will I get to meet him?"

" I don't know about this visit. But if we continue to see each other, of course you will soon."

"Enough of all this. I want the scoop, girlfriend! Keep me in the dark no longer!"

Lela happily began spilling the details to her friend.

Chapter Three

*L*ela was checking her make up for the tenth time when the phone rang. "Hello?"

"Hi, it's me. I'll be there in about five minutes."

"Are you okay? You sound funny."

"Is there somewhere we can talk alone when I get there?"

"Sure, I guess. Henry, you're scaring me. Are you mad at me?"

He sighed. "No, of course not. But I have to show you something and you won't like it."

"All right." She hung up, her heart beating rapidly. As she walked into the kitchen her mother glanced up at her. "Honey, what's wrong? You look troubled."

"That was Henry. He sounded upset. He has to show me something I won't like and wants to see me alone when he gets here." She absent-mindedly rubbed her stomach where the pain lay.

"I'll just stay in the kitchen until you let me know the coast is clear." She squeezed Lela's arm reassuringly. "It's probably nothing."

"Maybe. I guess I'll know soon. I hear the car now." She hurried to the front door.

Henry was getting out, an overnight bag and a sack with gifts in his hand, and a newspaper tucked under his arm. Ted was driving the

SUV. Henry nodded as Ted rolled up the window, backed out of the drive and was gone.

Lela opened the front door and watched Henry approach. As he stepped up on the porch, he smiled, and switching his overnight bag and gifts over, gave her a one armed hug. He glanced behind him, as though scanning the area. She moved back to allow him entry, then closed the door. "What in the world is the matter?" She asked as they walked into the den. Henry sat the gifts and his overnight bag down and turned to her. "Sit." He sat next to her. He held a newspaper "rag" in his hands.

"This is trash. It's *worse* than trash. I'm used to it, or I thought I was. I told you they make up vile stuff, especially about *me*, for some reason. Maybe it's because I try to be a good guy and I'm pretty boring, so they fabricate outlandish garbage in an attempt to outdo each other. I don't know." He bowed his head. "But this isn't all exactly made up. It's just redone."

He opened the paper and handed it to her. Lela looked down and gasped. She grabbed the paper and held it close to her face. "Who did this? *How* did they do this?"There was a full two-page photo spread. Henry standing behind her, his hands up her blouse. A full body slam embrace. Pose after pose that in reality had been full of sweet innocence, now appeared as twisted vulgarities. The headlines screamed, "*Now Hank's Robbing the Cradle.*" The article claimed very reliable sources reported young Lela Sawyer was Hank's new heartthrob, even though she was a seventeen-year-old high school student. They accused Hank of taking advantage of her and using her to cover up his real sexual addictions and choices.

"Oh, God!" She cried out. Tears spilled down her cheeks. "How could they say this? What did they do to make the pictures look this way?"

Henry pointed to the pictures. "They're altered by computer programs. Apparently some slug was hiding and taking pictures of us around the hospital and airport and then they doctored them up. I'm so sorry, Lela." He paused for a moment, then blushed as he looked her in the eye. "And just for the record I don't have any sexual addictions or perversions. I'm just a regular guy who made the mistake of telling a popular magazine I thought sex outside of marriage was wrong and

I'd decided to wait. Since then I've been a target." He smiled weakly. "The bars in New York have even named a non-alcoholic drink after me. '*Virgin Fields*', they call it."

She fell to his shoulder and cried. How dare they do this to her? How dare they do this to him? "They have no right to do this! Can't you sue them?"

"I've talked to my attorneys. I can sue. But these rags say and do stuff to all celebrities and suing simply gives them more publicity. They thrive on lawsuits. It's another way to get attention." He gently lifted her face to his. "I thought about doing a little background checking myself, after reading this, but that just felt wrong. So now I have to ask. How old *are* you, Lela?"

"Eighteen and a half."

He yelped. "Eighteen?!" His voice went up a full octave.

"And a half."

"And a half. Oh dear Lord." He put his head in his hands.

"How old are you, Henry?"

His voice came out muffled from between his hands. "Twenty nine." He paused. "And a half."

"Oh." Her voice was barely above a whisper.

"I thought you were older," he moaned. "You talked about getting your degree and working part time -"

"I was talking about my high school degree." Her voice sounded small and shocked.

He looked at her, finally. "Why didn't you tell me?"

"*Me*? I thought you were, like, twenty-one or twenty- two."

"I can't believe I have fallen for a child." He paused. "Furthermore, I can't believe I just said that out loud – I mean, I did, didn't I?" He asked, clearly hoping he hadn't.

"*Child?*" Lela stood, fists clenched. "I am not a *child*. I have been through more in the last year than most *adults*. Don't you dare call me a *child!*"

Henry stood up by her. "You're a teenager for cryin' out loud! They *chase* me and giggle. I thought you were in your twenties! A woman! Not a girl."

"Ohhhhh, you make me so mad! I'm eighteen years old, that *is* a woman!"

"Don't forget the 'and a half.'"

They stared at one another, nose to nose, breathing heavily. At that moment, Lela's father swung open the door. "Hey guys. Everything okay in here?"

They glared at him and shouted, "YES!" simultaneously.

He raised his eyebrows. "Alrighty then. Just let me know if you need a ref." He grinned and closed the door behind him.

Lela said between clenched teeth, "I want to knock you down so badly."

"See how mature you are? Such grown up talk."

She hit him on the arm. He grabbed her hand. She hit him on the other arm. He grabbed her other hand. Then he kissed her, hard. He dropped her hands and sat down on the couch. "Great, now I'm a child molester." Pause. "And I bet I said *that* out loud too." He fell over on his back and she jumped him.

"I swear, if you say I'm a child again I'm gonna beat you up."

He looked at her, and try as he might, could not help bursting out in laughter. "What a bloomin' mess. You sure move quick for a cripple."

"The nerve block helped." She said tersely.

"Please, Miz Lela, don't beat me up. I beg of you." He laughed again.

She realized she was straddling him with a pillow raised over her head ready to strike and blushed furiously. She quickly got up but when he tugged on her hand, she slumped down by him. "What are we going to do?"

"I don't know. Could your parents know about the age thing?"

"Well," she said dryly, "I am their child, so I suppose they know how old I am."

"Yeah, but do they know how old *I* am?"

"I don't think so." She shrugged. "I guess they'll know soon enough." She smiled sweetly. "Shall we join them in the dining room?"

Henry laughed again. "I guess, but you need to wipe that smeared lipstick off your face."

She smirked at him. "Afraid you'll get arrested?"

"Very, very funny. I think I'll just find a nice high cliff and jump off it. Save everybody a lot of trouble. My publicist is gonna kill me anyway." He stood up. "But you know what? I don't care. I like you." He held out his arm. "Come with me. Let's eat. Then we'll tell your parents I'm signing up for Social Security retirement and go from there. How's that sound?"

"Interesting." She put her arm through his and they walked through the swinging door into the kitchen to face her parents.

After dinner, the four of them sat around the dining table in silence. Henry had explained the situation, ending in showing them the gossip rag. Lela's mother had cried a little, saying she was dreading what everyone would say, then brought everyone to laughter when she realized she'd do some confronting about what her friends were reading. Both were surprised at Henry's age, but both agreed that Lela was mature for hers. They also pointed out to Henry that even though Lela was only eighteen, she *was* eighteen and could make up her own mind.

Henry looked relieved and shyly asked if that meant he was welcome to stay the few days as planned and "court" their daughter. Lela rolled her eyes and turned to Henry, "Are you going to ask them to hire a chaperone for us while we sit in the parlor?"

Henry looked innocently at Lela's father. "Would you do that, sir?"

"Why, certainly Henry. Do you prefer a portly gentlemen sitter or a stately lady sitter?"

"Well, let's see. Lela, how do you feel about it?"

"I feel like I'm gonna hurl."

"In that case, perhaps you could find someone who has a nursing background." They all laughed as Lela slowly got up and with great dignity walked out of the room.

They rented a movie and had all settled in the den with popcorn and drinks when Henry's cell phone rang. He excused himself and was gone for several minutes. Just as Lela had decided to check on him, he re-entered the room.

"That was my publicist." He sat down facing them. "She's adamant that I hold a press conference. All the legitimate newswires are picking up the story and "*Famous People*" has already called asking for an interview. They usually ignore the rags, so that tells me they know there's at least a grain of truth in all this." He paused for a moment to gather his thoughts. "I guess she's right. I can't ignore it. If it's something that's gonna be talked about, it seems I should be the one doin' the talkin'." He turned to Lela. "Before I do this, I want us to be very clear on what I'm going to say. I also want to be clear on what I'm *not* going to say. Sometimes that means more than the other."

"When are you going to hold the press conference?" Lela asked.

"Day after tomorrow. They can run a feed here, if that's okay. Just put me where the backdrop is neutral so no one will know where I am. My publicist will fly in that morning and go over everything. The tech guys will show up about two hours before the press conference." He looked at Lela's parents. "If it's all too much, just tell me. I don't want to take advantage of your hospitality."

They glanced at each other and Lela's father spoke. "Henry, I don't know where the relationship between you two might be headed. I do know what I see when you look at each other. Based on that, it seems to me that we need to get used to a little celebrity inconvenience from time to time. Have it here. We'll deal with it."

"Thanks. Let me call her back then we can watch that movie."

Henry left the room. Lela looked at her parents. "Are you sure this is okay with ya'll?"

"Honey, Henry is a nice boy and he cares about you. This isn't his fault and I don't want it to appear we believe any of it or that the minute there's a problem we aren't supportive. But are *you* comfortable with all this?" Her mother asked.

"I don't know. I am just so angry that he's treated unfairly. I haven't even considered what it may mean to me." She thought a minute. "It does kind of scare me to think my life might suddenly change so much. He lives in a fish bowl, doesn't he?"

Henry came back into the room. "It's all set for day after tomorrow, three o'clock. Hold onto your hat folks, this ought to be good." He plopped down on the couch next to Lela. "I'm ready for some fantasy entertainment that doesn't include me. Let's watch the movie, shall we?" He reached for Lela's hand and didn't let go.

Henry stood behind a borrowed podium with notes in front of him and waited for his cue. At the tech's nod, Henry began his speech. "I want to make a brief statement about the lies that were published in *"The Tattletale"* last week. Generally I don't respond to garbage, but since this has legal implications, I wanted to straighten things out for the record. First, I firmly believe my private life is nobody's business. I am in this field because I love to sing and entertain people, not because I think it's everyone's right to know what I do 24/7. I have always striven to be the kind of person parents would be happy for their children to look up to, and I figure dating said children wouldn't be much of a role model." He grinned, and the tech and film folks chuckled. "I am *not* dating an underage person. She is an adult. Of course the pictures that accompanied this accusation were altered to make me look <u>much</u> friendlier than I really was." More laughter from off camera. "I understand I can't control what these rags say about me, or how they might alter a photograph any way they desire. I have also come to understand people may choose to believe what some rag says, instead of what I say. I mean, come on, it's obvious folks at *"The Tattletale"* know a whole lot more about me than I know about myself, right?" He smiled again. "So, ultimately, the only thing I can do for my own sanity is to be sure that people who actually know me, care about me and whose respect I crave, know the truth. And the truth is this: I will *always* attempt to honor the God who saved me. I will try to represent Him well. I will fail from time to time, as we all do, but I gave myself to Him a long time ago. And that, ladies and gentlemen, is a real fact." He paused for a moment, looking straight into the camera. "Before dark I'll be made fun of for saying what I just said. Much of what I have said in the past has been made fun of because I'm just. Not. Cool. But ya know what? I don't really care and I sure don't apologize for my faith. Christ never apologized, and neither will I."

He turned to the moderator to indicate he was finished so the lines could be cleared to take questions from reporters stationed at various places around the country. The first question came from a young reporter that Henry didn't know. "So, Hank, exactly how old is 'this girl'?"

"My Mama taught me it is never polite to tell a woman's age. If you want to know, risk your life and ask the lady yourself." Everyone laughed.

The next question was from Nancy Blake, a reporter who had always treated Henry fairly. Her voice held warmth when she asked, "Hank, of course everyone wants to know, are there wedding bells in your future?"

"Well, Nancy, I certainly hope so someday, but the tux hasn't been rented."

The next reporter had a cocky look about him and clearly liked the camera. "Let me ask you plainly, are you and 'this Lela' planning on getting married?"

Henry asked, "You mean to each other?" Laughter.

"Yeah," the reporter answered, "To each other."

Henry said, "I haven't known her long enough to give you an answer. Who knows if she'd even have me? I like her a whole lot, though." Then he looked all excited and said, "Oh, and before you ask, her parents like me!"

Afterwards, Henry and his publicist sat and chatted. As she left, she thanked the Sawyers for the use of their home. She shook Lela's father's hand. "Sir, I promise all staff have been advised it won't be prudent for their careers if they chose to share the whereabouts of this house."

As if by some silent agreement, they all trudged into the den and collapsed as the last technician made his exit. "Lord, I'm glad that's over." Henry sighed. "I hate stuff like that. Makes me wish sometimes I was doing something – *anything* – but this."

Lela raised her head off the couch. "Don't say that, Henry. You know you're doing what you're supposed to be doing. Bad comes with every job, right?"

"Yeah, I guess." He looked over at her parents. "I appreciate your support. Maybe this will make 'em back off, but don't count on it." He shook his head in resignation. "Every time I think I'm used to this mess and that nothing can bother me anymore, they prove me wrong. Just help me remember that what I said should be what I mean."

"Agreed." Lela's father said. "I am very impressed with how you handle things with humor. You tell folks it's none of their business in the nicest way and they like it. I think I need lessons."

"When you're a skinny kid who likes music you better learn how to make people laugh or the bullies eat you for breakfast." He stretched. "Man, I'm beat. What say we call for pizza – I'll buy."

"None of us are gonna be skinny for long if you stick around."

"I'm the junk food king. It comes from livin' on the road. I promise to do better tomorrow, but today, let's celebrate."

That evening Lela and Henry were alone. She curled up by his side, head on his shoulder, his arm around her. He confessed his own concerns regarding their age had not lessened. "It's just such a huge gap. When you're my age I'll be nearly forty."

"And when you're eighty one I'll be a mere seventy. What will the neighbors think?"

Henry laughed. "You have a point." He looked down at her. "I don't *want* it to make a difference. I'm just afraid at some point you'll look at your young self in the mirror, look at my middle aged self and say '*What was I thinking? Where is the young guy we hired to clean out the pool?*' and pffft, you'll be gone."

Lela slugged him on his arm. "Thanks for the vote of confidence. Obviously true love has everything to do with the way we look, right?"

"Of course not, but-"

"And obviously, that means, if something else happens to me and this time I'm scarred horribly on my face, or become paralyzed or worse, you'll drop me like a hot potato, right?"

"No." Henry said quietly. "But our history is different too. I remember stuff that happened before you were born. I'll be talking about something and you'll look at me with a blank stare because you won't have a clue what I'm saying."

"Eh, that'll happen anyway. Guys and girls are so different, a lot of time our worlds are in different universes. We have a lot in common. We're both southerners, our social and religious beliefs are the same, we both have strong family ties. I think it's those kinds of things that help people stay close." She looked up at him. "Henry, it just occurred to me, we're both wrong."

"How so?"

Lela sat up. She took his hands in hers. "Speaking of religion, shouldn't we be letting God decide about us? We agree He put us together for a reason. He knows what the reason is. Why can't we just pray to be obedient? Does anything else really matter?"

Henry took Lela in his arms. "I may be the oldest, but you may very well be the smartest."

Chapter Four

The next day after breakfast, Lela reminded Henry of their conversation before his arrival. "When you called you said you had some exciting news you wanted to share. With all this other stuff, I forgot all about that."

"Oh, yeah! See what stress does for you? Makes you forget the good stuff. I'll be right back." He returned with a thick manila envelope and sat it in her lap.

"What's this?"

"What you have there, darlin', is a script. I've been asked to do a voice audition for an animated film for Disney."

"Henry! Congratulations! You must be so excited. Who would you play?"

"A very southern hound dog, what else?" He laughed. "Thank God he's a singin' hound dog, huh?"

Lela giggled. "Is his name Goober?"

"No, smarty pants, it ain't. His name is Beauregard. Bo for short."

"Of course. What are you chances, do you think?"

"I don't know. My manager says I'm a shoo-in. I've done a few things for them and everybody was really nice to me. But this is a pretty big deal." Henry sighed. "Let's face it, I'm not cut out to be a rocker for the long haul. I don't do drugs, I don't drink hard, I don't have sex with every groupie that tags along; I don't fit the M.O. at all. It seems like I tic off people because of that and they try to drag me through the mud with made up stuff because of it. I don't mind that so much for me, but I do mind it for my family and for the causes I support. And now you." He looked up at her. "I will not stand for you to be lied about. I have been able to keep my mouth shut about a lot, just shrugged stuff off as if it didn't matter. I'm not willing to do that if it's about you."

"Henry, I'm a big girl, I can take it."

"Really? Can you take it if they say I'm out partying with your best friend and sleeping with your first cousin and they have pictures to back it up? Can you take it if they say I not only have girlfriends but boyfriends too? Can you take it if they say they know I'm secretly huffing gas or mainlining heroin?" He ran his hand through his already seriously messed up hair. "Can you take it when we might have to be separated for weeks on end if you have a job or a class and you can't be on the road with me if I tour across the country? Or across the ocean? It's a very competitive business. Even if I don't feel like I'm competing with any one person, if I want my career to stay big I have to work hard and push myself in the limelight. Not just performing, but showing up at parties I hate with people I don't approve of and watch them do stuff that makes me sick. And I have to do it with a smile on my face, play nice. All the while they look down their noses at me and laugh behind my back because I am just too good to be true. The truth is, they believe they are so much better than me." He sat down next to her. "*Truth* is, they wouldn't *know* the truth if it bit them on the behind."

Lela placed her hand on his back. "Do you hate it so much you want to give it all up? Can you even do that?"

"Not yet. I have too many obligations toward a lot of people to walk off. But I do want to re-direct some of what I do and get some control of where I have to go and who I have to be with. I've put my foot down a lot, and sometimes it hasn't gone over too well. I've never been a yes man, no matter how powerful or rich someone might be. All this felt like it was coming to a head anyway. Then I met you." He turned to her. "You're all I think about. If someone is talking to me about recording a song, or performing on a show or doing this movie,

I'm thinking *'Can Lela make it? Can she be there?'* I walk into my own house and wonder *'Will Lela like this house? What kind of furniture does Lela like? Does Lela even know what kind of furniture she likes yet?'* I mean, when I was eighteen I didn't think about furniture at all! Do you?" Before she had a chance to respond, he kept on, "So now I have this urgency to get stuff in place so I can be more stationary in my work and be able to have a future like I want, not like the record company dictates. But I also have to face the fact that if I push too much, too far, I may not *have* a record company. And I'm not sure I care. Lela, I truly want God's will in my life. I may not know what that is all the time, but I sure do feel like you're a part of it."

"Thank you, Henry. I think about you all the time too. I've never felt like this before. It's kinda scary. But you're the one who has so much at stake. I don't want to mess anything up for you."

"Ah, that's not it at all. I mess up stuff pretty good on my own." He grinned at her. "I don't want to mess up stuff for *us,* though. Would you care if I suddenly could say to heck with it and be a music teacher after all?"

"Who, me? Remember, I'm the girl who had no idea who you were or what you did just a few short weeks ago. I don't care what you choose to do as long as you're sure it's what God wants for you. No guts, no glory, I say."

"I've been financially smart, and I have money enough to live off the rest of my life, if I'm careful. But if I didn't, would you be willing to live off a teachers salary?"

"I have so far. I don't seem to have suffered much for it. Look, Henry, I'm not saying I want to live in a cardboard box. I want to have a home and be able to pay the bills and go on vacation sometimes. But the kind of wealth you've seen isn't even real to me. I couldn't possibly miss it because I've never had it. I've never dreamed of being rich or longed for the easy life. It's not an issue with me. This is totally your call. Totally your life. I care for you so much, and if this is the real deal and we, uh, get married or something, it won't matter what your profession is."

"Honest?"

"Honest."

"Okay. I'll just keep prayin' about it. I figure if the Lord wants me to stay, He'll show me the way. And if He wants me out, He'll show me the way out. Meanwhile, want to look at this script with me?"

"Oh, yeah. Who do I get to be?"

"Lily. She's a cute little southern bulldog. I think Bo has a crush on her."

"Works for me. Let's get started."

That night, when Henry couldn't sleep, he found himself slipping to the floor to his knees. He placed his forehead on the old quilt, feeling the cool fabric soothe his brow. For several minutes he was still and silent, listening, searching for the place in his heart where he knew the Holy Spirit was waiting. Soon he felt the comforting stir as he allowed The Spirit to come to the front of his consciousness and Henry began to relax. "Hey, Lord," he whispered. "I figured I needed some serious time with You. I know You are not a God of fate or coincidence. I know You put Lela in my path. I know You have placed feelings in my heart for her that I would not have chosen to have. She's so *young*, Lord! I'm trying not to question You, but who am I kidding? You know the press is having a field day with this, and that's the least of it. I may not be the most mature twenty-nine year old on the planet, but I *am* twenty-nine. She's eighteen, Father! Still a kid in so many ways. Yet I feel so – so – attached to her. I feel like she belongs to me, Father." Overcome with emotion he began to cry. "Tell me what to do here, God. I'm afraid for her, I'm afraid for me. I don't wanna mess up. Do I allow myself to love her as much as I want to love her? Or do I hold back for now – sayin' that I can?" He shook his head. "I feel totally out of control, Lord." Realization dawned on him. "I guess that's what this is all about, huh." Henry nodded. "So that's it. You've placed me in a situation and I'm not in control. I guess that means You are and I should just shut up."

'Let not your heart be troubled. Be still and let Me fight these battles for you.'

"Yes, Father. I will. Thank You for loving me. I so don't deserve it. But thank You." Henry got up and crawled into bed. He was asleep instantly.

He awoke to a light tapping on his door. He rolled over and croaked, "Come in."

Lela peeked in. "Are you decent?"

"Nope but I ain't naked. Come on in." He sat up and pushed his hair out of his face. "What you got there?"

She sat down on the edge of the bed and he stuck his nose in her hair. "Your hair looks like cinnamon and smells like chocolate." He hugged her a little as she handed him one of the two cups she held.

"Hot chocolate it is. I hope you like it. Nobody else is up and I don't know how to make coffee."

Henry hid his smile in the cup. "This is great. You don't drink coffee?"

"Nope. I've tried it a few times but it's a no go for me. Mama says she didn't start drinking coffee till she was thirty and that was only because Daddy was a bad influence on her."

"This is just as good, if not better." He took a sip. "Why are you up so early?"

"I don't know." She looked at her lap. "Henry, I have been really praying about all this. I'm afraid and I feel like everything is out of control."

He laughed. "No joke. You musta been havin' the same prayer session I was havin' last night." He put his arm around her. "We aren't in control. I realized last night that's why it is so scary. God has rolled this into motion and it's certainly not what I expected. But since He doesn't make mistakes, I have a feeling we're gonna be fine, regardless."

Lela smiled. "Yeah, I know." She paused. "I just hope I don't embarrass you."

"*Embarrass* me? How on earth would you ever do that?" Henry sounded genuinely puzzled.

"Well, for all my bravado about my age, I know I'm still very young. Most everybody still considers me a kid." She nudged him. "Of course, a lot of them still think of you as a kid too, so don't feel all smug about it." She glanced up at him and he smiled. "But I realize you have some adult years and experience I don't have. Even if you had stayed your course and continued to teach, you'd be well into that profession. So you have something I don't have. And I can't change that. I don't want to feel inferior, but I do." She sniffed and Henry realized she was crying.

"Your age doesn't make you inferior, Lela. It just makes you less experienced. I've had voice students who were far younger than you and far superior to me in voice. Age has nothing to do with that. Look," He tilted her chin up so she was eye to eye with him. "God would never put you or me in a position so that one of us would be superior. He is The Superior One and we are to look to Him for everything. If our relationship continues down the path and I become your husband I promise you I will never lord over you. I will do my best to guide you as God directs. But honey, I don't have a superior bone in my body. Okay?"

Lela leaned into him and put her head on his shoulder. "Okay." She paused for a moment "Oh, Henry, I think I've fallen in love with you." Then she really cried.

He took her cup and set both of their hot chocolates on the nightstand. He pulled her into his arms and rocked her. "Well, that's a good thing darlin' cause the feelin' appears to be mutual. But I think it's a little soon to ask you to marry me."

He heard a muffled giggle. "Not if Daddy finds me in here on your bed in your arms."

Henry yelped like he'd been stung. "Girl, you're gonna cause us to have a shotgun wedding if you don't get out of here. I've been set up, I tell ya!" They both collapsed into a fit of giggles.

Lela stood up and got their cups. "Get up, lazy. This is your last day here. We must have stuff to do. And if we don't, get up anyway!"

"Yes ma'am. Just leave and I will." Lela turned to go. "Hey- since you don't make coffee, do you cook breakfast?"

"Sort of. I can make toast and cereal. Is that good enough?"

Henry sighed. "For starters. Go. Start. I'll be there in a few." He grinned as he watched her go. "Looks like I'm doomed to have a child bride." He shook his head. "Lord, what did I do to deserve this?" Henry looked heavenward. "Whatever it was, thank you!" He hopped out of bed and headed for the shower.

Bags packed, coat on, Henry stood outside Lela's house, Lela standing beside him. Her parents said their good-byes inside; leaving them alone for the few minutes it would take for Ted to turn the corner in the SUV. He called and was minutes away from the house. For the first time Henry felt awkward and wasn't sure what to say or do. He looked shyly at Lela. "I'm gonna miss you."

"I'll miss you too." She glanced down at her hands. "Time went by way too fast, you know? I guess I didn't give much thought beyond this point. I didn't realize it'd be here *now*."

"It does have a way of movin' on."

"So, what's next for you?" Lela asked.

"I'm hoping to spend some time with my folks and reacquaint myself with a few buddies. I've got some promotional stuff to work on, and a few visits I want to do for charity without the press hanging around. Other than that – oh, and spending every spare moment on the phone to you – I'll wait for Disney to call. I'm not scheduled for any shows or concerts right now. This is my down time."

"You'll let me know as soon as Disney says yes, won't you?" She lightly placed her hand on his chest.

"Or if they say no. This would be so great, though. I know I'll come off sounding lame, but this is something I've always thought about. You know, growing up with the movies and all, I used to think how fun it would be to talk for one of the characters."

"You're right, that does sound a little strange." She teased.

"What do you expect from a goober?"

"Too true. But seriously, I hope you get the part. I can tell everyone I have a boyfriend that ain't nothing but a hound dog." Suddenly her smile faded, and her hand dropped to her stomach.

"What's wrong, Lela?"

"Just my belly. Or, as the doctors say, my back." Lela's eyes misted up. "I'm going to miss you so much."

"Hey now, if you start cryin' I will too, and you know grown men aren't supposed to cry. It's sissy and all."

"I can't help it." She sniffed. "I guess it's the cold air."

"Yeah. It's rough on the eyes." Henry put his hands on her shoulders. "Come here, you. Give me a hug before Ted drives up and makes fun of us." He took her in his arms, his hand cradling her head. "Lord, you smell good." He closed his eyes, trying to imprint this moment in his mind. "I won't know what to do without you being around."

She looked up at him, eyes brimming. "I really hate this. I don't want you to go."

He smiled and bent down to kiss her. When they parted Henry's eyes were a bit too shiny. His voice was husky. "Maybe it won't be a long, long time before we can be together more. I know we don't need to rush things, but-" Ted blaring the car horn as he pulled into the driveway interrupted him. "Ah, I knew he'd show up too soon." Henry fiercely hugged Lela once more before he bent to pick up his bags. "I'll call you before bedtime."

"All right."

"Take care, sweetie. I think I may love you, Lela."

"You take care too. I think I may love you, Henry."

He jogged to the car, threw his bag in the backseat and climbed into the front. Ted waved to her and backed out of the driveway. She watched Henry wave till the car crested the hill, then they were gone.

Chapter Five

*L*ela walked back into the house and her Mother stood to wrap her arms around her. "Think you'll live?" She asked and smiled.

"I'm not sure. Did you feel empty when you had to leave Daddy?"

"Every time. I miss him now when he isn't home. Boy, do I remember how 'love sick' feels! People romanticize it in books, but it never felt romantic to me, just lonely. I was always impatient to see him again."

"Yeah. But I don't want to waste my life either. I can't just walk around looking at my watch to see how much more time has to go by before I see him again." She plopped down on the arm of the couch. "So, what time is it again?" She grinned at her mother and they both laughed.

Mrs. Sawyer sat down next to Lela. "Can I be serious for a moment?"

Lela sat up straighter. "Sure, Mama. What is it?"

"This feeling of being in love, the way you feel now, I mean, is a very powerful thing. But it doesn't last, you know."

Lela looked confused. "If this doesn't last, what does?"

Kathi Harper Hill

"What you have now is an overwhelming, emotional earthquake that threatens to overtake all your being. Right?"

"Amen to that."

"That's a feeling and we call it falling in love. But the love that sustains, the love that does last forever, is not a feeling. It is a choice. Do you think God loves us because of the way we feel toward Him or even the way He feels toward us?"

"I hope not. Sometimes I don't know *how* I feel toward Him. Like when I was injured and all I've been through since. I'm ashamed, but sometimes I wonder why He would let me suffer so much. And when I look around me at the world I can't understand why He would continue to love anybody."

"But God *chooses* to love us. And we choose to love Him back, or choose not to. And He gives us that freedom of choice. That's why choosing love is so special. God could have commanded our love, I suppose, but what good would it have been? I can't command your father to love me, and even if I could, would I cherish that kind of love? But I do cherish the love he offers me. He chooses to love me when I'm sick, or crabby or no longer as young looking as I used to be. And I choose to love him right back."

"When you say it like that, it sounds even better than falling in love."

"You are right, smart daughter. It's deeper and wiser and stronger. You might fall in love many times, but if it's the real thing, the other will begin to develop. Marriage can be the right choice. God will direct that, if you allow Him to do so."

"I've been praying about it. Henry has too." She clasped her mother's hands. "Oh, Mama, all I know is I've never felt like this before. It scares me because of who Henry is."

"Who he is or what he does?"

"Well, what he does. That he's famous and really, really rich. I don't know that I want that. But if I want Henry, I can't just ask him to stop what he's doing and give away all his money, can I?" Lela asked, half jokingly, but looked earnestly at her mother.

"No, of course not. Henry has to do what God wants him to do. And money isn't a bad thing, Lela, if you don't let it rule your life. In fact, God can use it to help grow His kingdom."

46

"It's just nothing like I ever dreamed, or wanted. I guess I thought I'd meet some guy in college and we'd settle down and live a nice, comfortable, middle class life."

"Like you're used to?"

"Yeah, like I'm used to."

"God shakes us up sometimes and takes us right out of our comfort zone. Don't let that scare you."

"I try not to." Lela's voice trembled. "I don't want to leave you and Daddy."

"Oh, honey, you don't have to leave us. God's timing will be perfect. If Henry is the man for you to marry, you'll be fine." Her mother lifted Lela's chin and looked in her eyes. "You'll always be my daughter. We can never be separated in that way. We can talk on the phone, e-mail, instant message, visit, write, you name it! We won't ignore each other, no matter how rich you get to be or how far away you might have to go. Henry is a fine young man. He won't try to replace us. He'll come before us, and rightly so. But I don't think he'd ever try to keep you from us."

"I don't think so either, Mama. He loves his parents too. But I see how his life has been scattered all over and he told me about how homesick he is sometimes." Lela sighed. "I know I'm still a child in some ways. I'm all excited about going away to college one day and terrified of leaving for even a few days the next. How in the world could I possibly be thinking about marriage?"

"You two don't have a train to catch. You have plenty of time to let this relationship grow. Maybe you need to go to college first. Just pray, honey. Your father and I will too. And I suggest you and Henry do some praying together. God will lead you through this." She wiped a stray tear from Lela's cheek.

"Thanks, Mama." Lela hugged her one more time. "I'm going to take a soak in the tub. Music, bubbles and a good book, that's the ticket."

Lela's mother sat for several moments in the gathering dusk. She prayed that God would guide Lela and Henry would honor God's will. "She's my only child, Lord." She whispered.

Then she wiped a few of her own tears.

Henry leaned back against the car seat and closed his eyes. He tried to think of something other than Lela, but it was hopeless. "So, Ted, tell me this won't kill me."

"They say what doesn't kill you makes you stronger."

"How strong were you?"

Ted laughed. "Not very. I'm married, aren't I?"

"Does it ever get easier to leave one another?"

"No. Since I started traveling with you it's brought back how hard being separated is. Before hiring on as your bodyguard I stayed close to home, just taking on gigs that were in state. I had forgotten how lonely it can be when you're away from your mate."

"What made you change your mind and go on tours with me?"

"You, I guess. If anybody ever needed protecting, it was you." He saw Henry start to protest. Ted raised his hand in a stop gesture. "Let me finish. You're a good kid and you were very naïve. You still are to some extent, and I like that fine. I want to help you stay that way, to be honest. My wife and I discussed how I felt about you being my job, and she agreed it was the right thing to do. There aren't many really good people in this business. And for every good guy there are twenty-five sharks looking to take advantage. That's not going to happen on my watch. I know you have managers and agents and they do a good job. But they don't care about you like I do. You're almost like a son to me, Hank." He cleared his throat. "Well, I guess I've embarrassed you enough for one day, I'll shut up."

Henry was silent for a moment. He tilted his head sideways, poked Ted in the shoulder with his fist and said, "Thanks."

Lela picked up the phone on the second ring. "Hello?"

"I got the part."

Lela squealed. "Congratulations! I'm so proud of you! When did you find out?"

"About fifteen minutes ago. My agent called to negotiate the deal. I told her I'd do it for free, but she was pretty adamant I get paid." He paused dramatically. "There's more good news, too."

"What? Tell me!"

"How would you like you and your folks to spend a few days in lovely Florida, all expenses paid, at the most faboo amusement park in the world?"

"Really?"

"I kid you not, sweet one."

"When?"

"Next month. My folks are coming too. I'll get the dates to you by tomorrow so your folks can ask off work, if you think they'd like to do this."

"Oh, I think they'd likey big time. Henry, I'm so excited. I miss you so much it hurts!"

"I miss you too. I used to make fun of guys moonin' around over girlfriends. Payback is rough." Henry paused for a moment. "What if I come up next Friday morning and spend the day? If your folks will have me again, I'll treat everyone to dinner Friday night."

As soon as Lela hung up, the phone rang again. "Hello?" Lela heard crying on the other end. "Emmie? What's wrong?"

"Oh, Lela, I'm really, really sorry. I just thought I was sorry before."

"What are you talking about?"

"I s-saw the tabloid about you and Hank." She hiccupped into the phone. " I know it's not true, because I know you. I understand what you were saying now."

"Yeah. It's pretty awful stuff. Henry did a press conference with the entertainment shows. *'Famous People'* was here, so I guess they'll cover it too."

"I feel like I'm in an alternate universe. My Lela is talking press conference and *'Famous People'* like it's just a normal every day thing."

"It doesn't feel that way. I just hope they clear this up. Henry says nothing stops the tabloids. He says laws will have to change in order for them to be stopped."

"I've got to do a paper in lit. class and I think I know what I'm going to do it on: *'Trash Journalism: It's time to take it out.'* Whaddya think?"

"Sounds brilliant. Go for it!"

"I believe I will. Did your visit go well?"

"Yes."

"Oh, Lela, you're falling in love, aren't you?"

Lela sighed. "I think so. I'm happy and scared. There are so many complications!"

"Yeah, well, you know God is bigger than any silly complications. If that's what He wants for ya'll, it's a done deal, so stop worrying."

"Thanks for being my friend, Emmie. Keep it all in your prayers."

"I will. I always do. His perfect will for my imperfect friend. I love you. Gotta go. Talk to me soon."

"Alright. Oh, wait!"

"What?"

"Henry may be coming up Friday. Just for the night, but maybe you could meet him then?"

"Oh, no!" Emmie wailed. "The only weekend I'll be out of town for a million years! I have to go to my cousin's baby shower in Savannah. Promise me, Lela, that I can meet him the next time."

"It's a promise. Take care, Emmie."

When Henry hung up, he immediately dialed his parents' home. "Hey Mama. It's your favorite son."

"And my only son. How are you, honey?"

"I'm good. I talked to Lela and she thinks her parents will want to go to Florida too. This will give you all a chance to get to know each other."

"Maybe it will work out." Henry's mother paused, choosing her words carefully. "I know you've talked to your daddy about this. And I know from what you've said to me you think this relationship is serious. If it does lead to marriage, Henry, I want you and Lela to wait for a while."

"We're trying not to rush, Mama. But it's all I can do not to drive to her house every day instead of thinking about music or what I need to do next in my career. It's like I'm possessed, or something."

His mother laughed softly. "Oh, yes, I remember those times. God can deal with those feelings just like He deals with all your other ones. If this is the real thing Henry, it will last and you can spend the rest of your life with her. Just don't jump into things too quickly."

"What's too quickly? Part of me feels like it's all in slow motion and I'm about to scream, and part of me feels like I'm movin' so fast I can't see straight." Henry raked his free hand through his hair. "I *have* to rely on God, cause I don't have any sense left."

"Well, be sure you do rely on Him. Lela is very young, and that worries me a bit. But if this is God's will, she will be the perfect age and the perfect wife for you."

"Her parents are nice folks. They put God in the center of their lives. Lela's young, but she has this calm nature about her that seems older than me sometimes. The young part of her makes me want to protect her and stuff. And then we kiss and I don't want to protect her anymore." Silence. "Wait. Did I, um, just say that last part out loud?"

"Yes."

"Sorry."

"Do you want to say anything else out loud?"

"No ma'am. I think I've said enough."

"I think so too. Be careful, Henry. It is your job to protect her, you know."

"I know, Mama. I will, I promise. I'll call you as soon as I have the Disney dates."

"I love you, son. Take care. Remember who you represent every day of your life."

"I do. I will. I love you."

Henry hung up the phone and hung down his head, shaking it back and forth. He really, *really*, needed to do something about thinking out loud. He wondered if there was a pill for that?

But he wondered it out loud.

Chapter Six

People smiled as they walked past the group who appeared to be having such a wonderful time while eating in the open-air restaurant. Occasionally someone would recognize the young blond man and start in surprise, pointing him out to their companions as they walked on by. No one bothered them, though. Everyone seemed to be of the like mind that it would be far too rude to interrupt that much fun.

All four parents, Ted, with his wife and small son, had joined Lela and Henry at the table and were having a blast. The laughter began when Henry's mother shared how embarrassed they were when Henry, at the age of three, escaped their pew during a funeral and stood in front of the casket singing '*Jeremiah was a bullfrog*' at the top of his lungs before they could stop him. The deceased, of course, had been named Jeremiah.

Lela's mother tried to top that story by relaying how they lost Lela in a department store. Fear had turned to total humiliation when Lela was found striking a pose in the big plate glass window facing the mall. She had carefully removed all her clothes before posing with the manikins; explaining she didn't have a bathing suit like they did and she wanted to swim. She burst into tears when she realized there was no water in the kiddy pool on display. They dragged her out of the mall, kicking and screaming, still naked.

Henry and Lela begged their parents to stop, but were pretty unconvincing as they were laughing as hysterically as everyone else.

Afterwards, walking back to the rooms, Henry and Lela held hands, her head on his shoulder. Their parents lagged slightly behind, talking with Ted and his wife. Ted's son lay in his father's arms, sound asleep.

"I love you, I love your mama, I love your daddy, I love Ted and his family, I love my folks, and I love Florida." Lela raised her head up. "Did I leave anything out?"

"Nope, I think you got it covered." He leaned down and kissed the top of her head. "I too love the above, and I really love your pretty red headed self."

Lela sighed. "God is so good. I never knew how much fun having a boyfriend could be. I think I'll keep you."

"I'd appreciate it. I've got a lot invested in this trip, you know."

"Hey, I thought it was free."

"Oh, yeah."

She playfully hit him on the arm. "You are such a big spender. I imagine you have the first dollar you ever made, right?"

"Um, no. The first dollar I ever made was spent on a video game I had been longin' for. When I got that first check from baggin' groceries, I thought I'd hit the lottery. Couldn't spend it fast enough."

"I've heard similar stories from friends. By the time I had a part time job other than baby-sitting, I was spending it on clothes and shoes. Then I got hurt and haven't had a dime since."

Henry spoke softly. "You tease about that, but you've missed out on a bunch, haven't you?"

"Yes. Sometimes I question God, but mostly I try to believe He may have saved me from some far greater thing by getting me out of the picture for so long. Plus, I wouldn't have met you in New York."

"I have a feeling no matter what, God would have put us together some way. It's just too right for it to be any other way."

They both turned as Henry's father called to them. "Wait up. We want to talk over tomorrow's plans."

They stopped and waited. As the rest of the group caught up, Lela held on to Henry's hand tightly.

She had never been so happy in her life.

The next morning before breakfast, Henry rang Lela's room phone. "I've got an idea. Although everyone's scheduled to go home in the morning, why don't you stay on? I have to be here a few more days to work on the script and meet with executives to talk about a video for charity. Ted will be here too, so it's not like we'll be alone. Well, him plus the several thousand people who show up here everyday. What do you say?"

"I don't know." Lela said slowly. "I'll mention it to Mama and Daddy."

"I'd be busy during the day, but that would still give us two evenings to eat together and stuff. My flight doesn't leave till around four the next afternoon, so we could play in the park half a day. We can rent movies or buy books to occupy you during the day, if you don't want to shop."

"Yeah, you know I won't feel like shopping," She said dryly. "And I can keep myself entertained, it's not that." She was silent for a minute. "It's just my parents, or yours, for that matter, may not like the idea."

"Oh." Henry sighed. "I keep forgetting your age. I've been an adult long enough that I don't think about getting my folks' permission to do something." He heard Lela start to protest. "I'm not saying you're not an adult. I ain't goin' down that road again."

"Good. But I still live at home. I've had to be taken care of by them, and I feel obligated to have their approval."

"I understand completely. Really, I do Lela. If you mention it and sense the least bit of resistance, don't fight. We've got plenty of time ahead of us. Just let me know what you decide."

"I'll mention it before we meet up. I'll do hand signals or something during breakfast if it's a no go."

"A nice slice across the throat with your finger will do just fine."

Lela laughed as she hung up. She knocked on the door between her suite and her parents', hand across her belly. "Ya'll about ready for to breakfast?"

"Just about. Your mother is drying her hair. What's up, are you starving?"

"No. Henry just called and wondered if I could stay the rest of the week. Ted's staying, of course, so it's not like we're here alone."

"Not to mention the thousands of people that visit each day."

Lela looked startled. "That's exactly what Henry said."

Her father smiled. "Are you asking my permission to stay?"

"I guess so."

He studied the floor for a minute. "Look, Lela, I think it's time for me to stop giving you permission to do things. You seem to be headed toward a fairly serious relationship, a very adult relationship. So, I guess we need to start treating you like an adult."

"Does that mean I can stay?"

Her father laughed and hugged her. "Well, you better ask your mother!"

"Ask me what?" Vicki inquired as she entered, arms full of curlers and a hair dryer.

"Henry wants me to stay for a few more days while he finishes up. Ted's staying too."

Her mother raised her eyebrows, looking at Lela's father. "And you said?"

"I said it was time we stopped giving permission. She's growing up and in an adult relationship, so she needs to make up her own mind."

"Agreed. Do you feel up to it? You'll be alright in a room alone?"

"I was in New York." Lela answered her mother's second question, ignoring the first.

"You're a big girl now. It's not a matter of us trusting you anymore, it's trusting yourself." She picked up her purse. "Let's go eat breakfast."

When they entered the restaurant, Henry caught her eye and gave her a quizzical look. She grinned and gave a thumbs up. Breakfast was loud and at one point, Jonathan, Ted's son, clamped his hands over his ears and propped his elbows on the table. Everyone stopped talking and burst into laughter.

"I guess Jonathan may have saved us from getting kicked out if we're that loud." Henry's father said.

"It will be quieter when all of you leave. I may be able to hear myself think." Henry said. "Ted isn't near as noisy without you, Susan."

Ted's wife smiled. "I inspire him to talk. He's afraid I'll say something embarrassing if I get a turn."

Ted looked stricken. "Not so, dear wife. You are by far the smarter of the two of us. I'd want you to stay if Jonathan wouldn't miss school."

"Good news, Ted," Henry spoke up. "Lela's staying with us."

Ted looked surprised. "Really?" He turned to Lela. "Aren't you afraid you'll get bored?"

"Henry says he'll make sure I'm entertained with movies and books during the day. He can feed me good food in the evenings."

Ted glanced at Henry. "That is if the meetings end on time and he gets a chance to leave before the middle of the night."

Lela shrugged. "I'm a big girl." She said, echoing her mother's sentiment. "I'll find something to do. It's only for a couple of days anyway."

Ted turned to Lela's parents. "I'll take good care of her right along with Henry. My cell phone stays on, and I'll be available when Henry isn't."

Henry watched as Lela's eyes narrowed. He knew what *that* meant. "Um, Ted, Lela appreciates that, I know. But I'm sure her parents understand she's capable of taking care of herself."

"Is that so?" Ted turned to Lela. "I didn't mean to make it sound like you couldn't take care of yourself. I just know this is a big place and we all need people we can depend on if we need them."

Lela's look softened. "Thanks. I appreciate it, Ted."

Henry's father spoke up. "Now, Henry, don't get all busy and forget she's here. I know how you are when you get focused on something, you tend to disregard other folks' feelings."

Henry looked at Lela with a *'See, my folks treat me like a child too!'* triumphant face, making her grin. "Yes, Daddy, I'll be a good boy and not forget Lela's here. I'll make a note and pin it to my shirt pocket."

Jonathan brightened. "Hey, my Mommy does that for me sometimes too!" He said. "Specially when I gotta member somethin' important."

Henry smiled at Jonathan. "Well, I'd say Lela's pretty important, wouldn't you?"

"She sure is." He agreed solemnly. As an afterthought, he added. "And she's pretty too."

Ted was taking everyone to the airport. Henry and Lela said their good byes at the hotel and were now sitting by the pool under a big umbrella, drinking lemonade.

"This is the life." Henry gazed out over the blue water of the swimming pool, and beyond to the ocean and sky. "I don't think you'll need movies or books. Just come out here and sit with your eyes closed. Think about me, inside a conference room, reading a script and then in an office saying yes sir and no sir to suits in order to get them to donate money for a charity video."

"You poor thing. Let's see how much sympathy I can come up with." She waited a few seconds. "Hmmm. None."

He flapped at her with his hand, but she dodged him. "I see the heat is makin' you sarcastic. Perhaps we should go in."

"Not a chance. I haven't felt this relaxed since I was still groggy from anesthesia." She adjusted the floppy brimmed hat she wore and settled further into the lounge chair.

Henry chuckled. "Now *that's* relaxed." He stretched and yawned. "Speaking of the suits, I have a meeting at three to look at some changes in the script. I asked how long the meeting would go, and they said," Henry's tone took on a nasal quality, " *'As long as it takes, Mr. Fields'.*"

Lela giggled. "Well, nothing like a definitive answer. If you don't make it back by seven I'll order a sandwich in the room and watch a pay per view. I looked at the guide, and there's actually two movies I want to see."

"Even if it's late, I'd like to peek in and say good night."

"Sure. I'll still be awake, probably. I'm a night owl. And if I go to sleep, knocking ought to wake me up." She looked at him. "But be prepared for fear. Waking me up ain't pretty."

"Yeah, makes me wanna cry." He stretched again. "What really makes me want to cry is gettin' up and goin'." He turned to Lela and took her hand. "You gonna stay here for a while?"

"I think I will. I have a book." She pointed to her tote bag. "I will read and doze some. You know, Henry, it's a good thing you're rich, I've decided."

"Why's that?"

"Cause I could get used to this." She smiled lazily.

"Wench, you'll work for a livin'. *And*, wait on me hand and foot as well as carin' for our twelve children."

"Isn't twelve a little excessive?"

Henry shrugged. "Well, I won't be carryin' 'em."

"Keep talking like that and you won't be able to sire them either."

"Ouch. With that I will go." Henry stood, shaking his baggy shorts away from his legs. He bent down and kissed her lightly. "Even though you got a mean mouth on you, I love you."

"And well you should." She smiled up at him. "Come back to me, cause I'll miss you." She lowered her sunglasses and they locked eyes for a moment.

"Will do." Henry's voice took on a husky quality as he cupped her face for a moment. Straightening again, he sighed heavily. "I'll get back as soon as I can." He rolled his eyes. "Whenever that is."

Lela watched him go. She did a little stretching herself, then reached in her tote for the new mystery novel and began to read, one hand drifting unconsciously to hold her belly.

Chapter Seven

*H*enry knocked softly on Lela's hotel room door. He grinned after several attempts and knocked a little louder. Finally the door opened as far as the chain would allow.

"Open up, it's me."

Lela undid the chain and stepped back for him to enter. Henry's grin widened as he looked at her. Her hair was a wild array of red tangles and the night-light caused golden sparks to fly about the curls. She had on a nearly knee length fan club t-shirt with his face spread all over the front. "Love your sleepwear."

"It's the latest fashion." Lela mumbled as she stumbled back toward the bed. "What time is it?"

"Two thirty. We talked a long time about the charity event before we even started reading the script." He walked toward her. "I knew you'd be asleep, but I just wanted to check in a minute and say good night. Were you terribly bored alone?"

"Nah, I was fine. I watched a movie and read some. You don't have to entertain me every second. I know you'll be busy most of the time." She was sitting on the edge of the bed, eyes half shut.

Henry sat next to her, and she dropped her head to his shoulder. He put his arm around her waist, and she snuggled closer. She was warm from sleep and he closed his eyes and took her in. She smelled so sweet. He felt her body relax against him, melting into his side. "Here, let me tuck you in, you're practically asleep sitting up." He stood and tenderly pulled the covers out from under her. She toppled over to her side. As he tugged on the covers, his hand brushed her hip.

And lingered there.

He found himself leaning over her and she turned her face to look at him. Her blue eyes looked black in the dim light and her lips were moist and open. Her hair fanned out on the pillow in a fiery mass. As he kissed her, his hand moved to the small of her back. He lay down beside her and she scooted closer to him. Her hands caressed his chest and he heard himself groan as his heart began to beat faster. He caught her hair up in his hands and kissed her face, her eyes, her mouth. She pressed closer to him, and electrified fire coursed through them. His hands slid around her waist and he felt a rush like nothing he'd ever experienced.

His cell phone rang.

They both jumped, and Henry stood straight up to wrestle the phone out of his jean pocket. He managed a strangled, "What!" into the phone.

"Where are you?"

"I'm in Lela's room. I- I just came by for a second to tell her good night before goin' to my room."

For the first time Henry could recall, Ted was silent on the other end of the phone.

"I'm okay, Ted."

"Sure you are." Ted paused for a moment. "Look, buddy, I'm not your dad, but I hope I am your friend. As an old married man, it sounds to me like you need to go to your room *now*." His voice softened. "If not for your sake, for Lela's."

Henry felt himself blushing. "Right. I'll be there shortly. I'll call you as soon as I'm locked in for the night."

"I'll wait for your call."

"Thanks, Ted."

"Anytime, Hank."

Henry snapped the phone closed, put it back in his pocket and sat on the chair next to the bed. He put his head in his hands. "I am so sorry, Lela." He looked up. "Can you forgive me?"

She snorted. "Right now I'm trying to forgive Ted."

Henry shook his head. "You better be thankin' the good Lord for Ted and his rescue." He rubbed his hands nervously on his jeans. "I cannot excuse my behavior. This shouldn't have happened! Thank *God* for Ted, or who knows what *would* have happened!" Henry stood and began to pace. "I've always been so self righteous about this sort of thing. I knew God had really protected me in a lot of ways, and I took it for granted. Then I waltz in here like I'm invulnerable and wind up acting like you're my midnight snack." He whirled and looked at her. "The one girl I've ever really cared about and I cave in a flash at the very first unguarded opportunity. Oh, yeah, I'm really Mr. Holier-than-thou, all right."

"Well, you didn't hear me complaining or trying to get you to stop, did you?" Lela asked.

"And that's supposed to make me feel better? Lord, Lela, I don't want to start blaming you! I shouldn't have even presumed I could be here and not take advantage of the situation." He looked down at the floor. "I've heard guys talk since I was fifteen years old. About how to get in a girls pants. How we're guys and can't help it. How it's okay if the girl says it's okay. And if she doesn't say it's okay, work on her till she does." He shook his head. "And you know what? I always felt I was way better than them. I figured if I stayed away from situations," He waved his hand around the room, "like this one, I could wait till I got married. Of course I didn't know I was gonna be single at nearly thirty." He sighed. "Of course, you'd think since I *am* nearly thirty I'd know better." He sat back down, spent.

By now Lela was sitting up in bed, covers up to her chin. Tears welled up in her eyes. "I've never felt this way before. Now look what I've done." She said in a small voice. "I'm sorry, Henry."

"Me too." He stood up. "I better go. We'll talk later." He started toward her, thought better of it and walked toward the door. "Good night, Lela."

"Good night, Henry." She watched him walk out the door, then flung herself into her pillow and sobbed. "Oh, Father, I messed up! Help us make it right again." She cried herself to sleep.

Henry unlocked his door and sprawled into a chair. He flipped open his phone and punched Ted's number. After one ring, Ted picked up. "You okay?"

"Nope. I'm a royal mess."

"Want me to come up?"

Henry hesitated for a moment. "Would you mind? I think I need to talk."

"I'll be there in five."

The phone went dead and Henry hit the floor on his knees. It was all he knew to do. "Lord, help me. Have I ruined it for us? I feel guilty because I am. Not just for takin' advantage of Lela, but for being so smug thinkin' I was strong enough to resist any temptation. Show me how to fix this, please." He heard a knock at the door. He got up and let Ted in.

"Ok, buddy, talk. I've got the rest of the night if you need it."

"What about sleep?" Henry asked.

"Highly overrated. Friendship is more important."

"Thanks." Henry turned toward the room. He put his hands on his hips and dropped his head. "I messed up tonight, Ted."

Ted closed his eyes. "How badly?"

Henry felt himself blushing again. "Well, we didn't get very far, if that's what you're askin'. No thanks to me. If you hadn't called, I'm not sure I could say that."

Ted let out his breath. "Thank God. When I called your room and you didn't answer, I felt such an urgency to check on you. I knew you had time to already be in you room. I thought something was wrong, I sensed you were in danger."

"You were right. Just maybe not the kind of danger you imagined." Henry ran his hands through his hair. "I don't know if I can face her in the mornin'. This mornin', I mean. I'm embarrassed and ashamed."

"Is she upset with you?"

"I think she's more embarrassed than anything. It all just happened. I know it's more my responsibility than hers. I'm the man, I should have acted more responsibly."

"Did you apologize to her?"

"Yeah. But when I left her room, I felt like we were damaged somehow." Henry blinked back tears. "How do I fix this? How do I know I won't act the same way the next time we're alone? How can I look her in the eye again?"

Ted walked over and patted Henry on the shoulder. "You're not the first couple to struggle with lust, you know."

Henry's face blazed red. "This is so embarrassin'."

"It's normal, Hank." Ted sighed. "When you're in the moment it feels so good and so urgent that you can lose control. Heck, you don't want control, you want *sex*. You've never said much, but I think you have tried to lead a decent life and this has surprised you, hasn't it?"

"Yeah." He glanced at Ted. "I'm embarrassed to talk to you about this. And I'm ashamed to say I'm embarrassed to tell another man that I'm still a virgin at the age of twenty- nine, though that's been a conscious decision, not lack of opportunity. Even though I said it in an interview, it's different to say it face to face to another man."

"Would it make you feel any better if I told you I wish I'd been a virgin when Susan and I got married?"

Henry looked at him cautiously, "Yeah?"

"She and I were sexually active before we got married. We were twenty- one when we met and both virgins. A year into the relationship we thought she was pregnant. I've never felt so scared or sick in my life." He paused for a moment deciding how much to share. "Turned out she *was* pregnant. But before we could think much about it, she lost the baby. I spent days, weeks, *months* grieving over that baby. And the guilt?" Ted swallowed hard. "If we'd waited till marriage, that baby would have never existed. None of that would have happened." He looked at Henry. "We love each other deeply, and our marriage is strong. But that almost destroyed our relationship before we had a chance to marry. If the wedding had not already been planned, I'm not sure we would have gone through with it. We were in so much pain." He shook his head. "We waited years to have a baby because of that pain. When Susan got pregnant with Jonathan, we were absolutely terrified that she would miscarry. Up until the day he was born healthy, we lived in fear." Ted took a deep breath. "God has a reason for everything He tells us. He tells us plainly that sex is for a husband and wife only. Did you know it's symbolic physically of the spiritual relationship we'll have with Christ? The union of one flesh like the union of one spirit with Him. And we treat it like a sports event."

"I'm so sorry about the baby, Ted. I never want to jeopardize any chance Lela and I might have and I sure don't want to start a family before marriage. I can't imagine how you felt." He looked earnestly at Ted for direction. "Should I go back to Lela and apologize again?"

"Not now. Wait till daylight. But you both need to forgive each other and yourselves." Ted thought a moment. "Look, Hank, this can be a struggle for you both. You need to set boundaries so this won't happen again. Don't kid yourself; it's going to be even more difficult now. You've had a taste and you're going to crave it. So is she. Now you have to be even more careful. You must be held accountable. I'll be glad to be one of those that will do that for you, but be aware you might get angry with me."

Henry looked surprised. "I won't get mad. I'll be grateful."

"Ha. Just wait. Satan will use lust and do his best to drive a wedge in our friendship if you ask me to take on this with you. He's found a natural foothold and he won't turn loose easily."

"Well, that makes me feel even worse." Henry hit his leg with his fist. "I *hate* screwin' up!" He hung his head. "I hate consequences, which is why I try to be so careful to start with. But I do want you to hold me accountable. Lela needs that too. When I talk to her, I'll make sure she's got a female she can ask to help." He looked at Ted. "I know I love her. I've never felt this way before. And I know the difference between the love I feel for her and the lust I felt for her a little while ago. It's weird. I've been attracted to her from the get go. But it was a sweet, powerful, protective feelin'. This is powerful too, but it's not very protective. It's greedy. And hungry. I want it and I like it and I hate it. So how can all that change after you're married?"

"God gave us sex as a gift. When you get married, you give yourself to your bride, including physically. It is powerful and overwhelming. But when you are in the sacred covenant of marriage, you can let go and be overwhelmed by it because she is yours and you are hers. There's nothing to fear, nothing to lose. You're not wrongly using one another. It's a way to bond and be as close as we can ever get to another person. She becomes you, you become her. One flesh, buddy." Ted looked at Henry intently. "It's worth waiting for. Don't let lust fool you. Let love guide you instead and the gift will be waiting for you."

"Thanks, Ted." Henry looked relieved. "Can we pray together before you leave?"

"Sure, buddy. Anytime."

After Ted left, Henry lay in bed thinking about the last thing Ted had said. *"Remember, love is more than a feeling. It's knowledge, a commitment, a choice. Lust is nothing more than a feeling."*

"Well, Lord," Henry began, "First I want to thank You for the lesson. Next I want to ask that I have enough sense to *learn* the lesson. I believe You've given me Lela. And if that's true, she's mine to protect. That means from myself too. I can't do it alone, Lord. I found that out! Lord, You know I'm a stubborn, hard headed idiot sometimes, and it's gotten me in trouble more times than once. So, Lord, please, please don't let me ignore Your warnings. Keep me strong and help me stay out of places where I will give into my feelings for Lela – who am I kidding? - feelings I want *for me-* because I know it's all just under the surface. Thank you for Ted. He's such a good man. Thank you for my parents; help me to never do anything to shame them. Or Lela's parents for that matter. I want them to love me, Lord, not wish me dead." He smiled slightly. "I thank you for Lela. Help me to honor her. Help me to honor You, Lord." Comforted by the Holy Spirit, Henry, as usual, turned on his side and went instantly to sleep.

Lela awoke to sunlight peeking at her around the closed curtains. For a moment she didn't understand the anxiety she felt, then it all came flooding back. She buried her head in her pillow, feelings of embarrassment and shame overcoming her. The way Henry had re-acted made her feel unclean. He was obviously ashamed, and that made her feel even worse. What must he think of her? She admitted she had desired him so badly that she had just given in to her body's longings and had been willing to do whatever he wanted. What was wrong with her?! She knew better and she'd never dreamed she would give in like that. And what did it take? Absolutely nothing. In seconds she was on fire and would have succumbed to it all. She was too ashamed to pray, so she just lay there, miserable.

Her bedside phone rang. She knew it had to be Henry. She wasn't sure she could talk. Slowly she picked up the phone. "Hello?"

It was her mother. She groaned inwardly and fought tears. "Good morning, sweetheart. Were you still asleep?"

"Just waking up, actually. I guess I should have already been up."

"You're on vacation, enjoy sleeping. We missed you and I wanted to speak to you before you left your room for the day. Are you and Henry having fun?"

Lela cringed. "He worked till the middle of the night, going over the script and working on charity stuff. He came by and told me good night around two or three. I haven't seen him this morning."

"Goodness. I guess he's still asleep. Aren't you going to get bored if his schedule stays like that?"

"I'm not bored. I entertained myself with a movie and a book. I figure we will have some time together this afternoon." *'If I can look him in the eye.'* She thought.

"Well, then, I hope you have a good time. I'll let you go. We love you. Oh! I almost forgot to ask, are ya'll still coming home Saturday?"

"As far as I know."

"Good. If Henry brings you home, maybe he can spend the night and go to church with us Sunday. I don't think the congregation will get too excited over him, he'll be safe from poor behavior there."

"I'll ask him."

"Lela, is everything all right with you and Henry?"

"Sure, why do you ask?"

"I don't know. You sound – odd."

Lela felt tears threaten again. "Oh, Mama." She began to cry. "When Henry came by last night, we kissed, and then we went too far. I've ruined it, I know I have! I'm so sorry." Lela shook with sobs.

There was silence on the other end for a moment. "Lela, calm down. Did you…"

"No, no. Henry's phone rang. It was Ted wanting to know why he wasn't in his room yet. Then Henry got all upset over what happened. He said he was sorry, it was his fault and he left. But it wasn't just his fault. It's my fault too. What's wrong with me? Why didn't I just stop everything before we were both embarrassed?"

Her mother sighed. "Because you're human. So is Henry. Have you talked at all since?"

"No. After he left, I finally went to sleep. It's true that I haven't spoken to him this morning."

"Honey, this is something you will both have to agree to not let happen again. It's a natural response when you become close to one another. Just don't get in situations where it can occur." She listened to Lela cry for a moment. "It's not the end of the world. You and Henry can work this out. Have you prayed about this at all?"

"I can't," Lela mumbled. "I'm too ashamed."

She could hear the smile in her mother's voice. "Well, guess what? God already knows. You must go to Him and repent. He loves you even more than I do, you know. He's already waiting on you with open arms."

"Oh, Mama, will you pray with me?"

"Anytime, sweetie."

After Lela hung up, she got out of bed, washed her face and took a deep breath. She glanced at the clock. It was almost ten. She knew Henry was probably still asleep, but she couldn't wait any longer to speak with him. She dialed his room and the phone rang several times. Just as she was about to hang up, she heard a fumbling noise, what sounded like Henry dropping the phone, and then more fumbling. "Wha – lo?"

Lela felt all her nervousness melting as her heart filled with affection and humor for this young man. "Wha-lo, yourself. Wake up. I've called to grovel and beg your forgiveness one more time and pray we can start this day with a clean slate."

"Hey Lela." He croaked. "Can you hold on a minute? Give me a second to wake up."

"Sure. Want to call me back?"

"No!" He sounded alarmed. "I don't want to lose connection of any kind. Just hold on. I'll be right back."

He put the phone down, and Lela prayed silently, '*Lord help us do this right. Help us to honor You and each other.*'

Henry came back on the line. "Sorry. Now maybe I can speak English."

"What language is 'wha-lo?'" She teased.

"The language of a sleeping fool. At least you're still speaking to me. Are you alright?"

"Yes. I know I asked your forgiveness earlier, but I'm asking again. Henry, will you please forgive me?"

"I feel ashamed that you even have to ask. This was all my fault, Lela. You trusted me and I took advantage of the situation. I want you to know I didn't plan it. Lord, if you'd asked me beforehand I would have said I would never let that kind of thing happen. Will you forgive *me*? I promise I won't let us get into a situation like that again."

"I do forgive you Henry. I want us to pray together and learn from this. And maybe we need to stop trying to blame ourselves and realize it was a joint mistake. Not just your fault or mine, but ours. Just like it's our responsibility to keep it from happening again." She paused and said in a small voice, "Because part of me wants it to happen again. If you don't help, who's going to protect me from *me*?"

"Oh, Lela, I know. I talked to Ted for a long time after I left your room and he said once we opened the door it makes it difficult to not keep opening it wider and wider. He says we need to be held accountable to others. He's going to do that for me, as embarrassing as it is."

"Mama said the same thing."

"Wait. You told your *Mama*? Well, we don't have to worry anymore, cause your daddy will kill me first chance he gets." He paused as though pondering. "I wonder what time his plane will land."

Lela giggled. "I don't know that she'll even tell Daddy. She didn't get angry. She just said we had to agree to not put ourselves in a situation where things can get out of hand. If Ted holds you accountable, I'll find someone for me too."

"It doesn't seem to me your mother is a good idea."

"I think I may ask my Bible study leader, Jean Smithfield. She's an older lady, and she has been pretty up front about sexual temptations in our studies. She would do it for me in an honorable way."

"She sounds like the right one to ask." He added, "Tonight I'm supposed to be finished by six. Be ready to go out to eat and we'll sit by the pool or something afterwards. I'll tell Ted what time we'll be in and I'll call him as soon as I get in my room. That way I know he's waiting on my call." Henry paused. "I feel like I'm on parole or something. But I'm not taking any more chances while we're down here. When we get back home, we'll have to set rules up." He sighed. "This feels like such a big deal. I don't know if I'm making it worse than it is, or if Satan wants me to feel that way so I won't be cautious."

"We'll make it a big deal for these next few days. We can get counsel back home and find out how to handle this. All I know right now is I'm so glad you're in my life."

Chapter Eight

When Lela returned home, she made an appointment to meet with Jean Smithfield as quickly as possible. A dark-haired, portly Mrs. Smithfield welcomed Lela into her home and led her into a light filled sunroom. The room was full of stained glass, potted plants and half hidden woodland figures, that peeked out from behind furniture, fountains and flowers. A fire blazed in a stacked rock fireplace and Lela could faintly make out some kind of music playing softly in the background. They sat on dark stained wicker upholstered with plump, tropical themed cushions. As they drank hot tea from delicate cups imprinted with old-fashioned tea roses, Jean listened to Lela's story, her plump, well-manicured hands grasping Lela's. She gave Lela a tissue when she cried and prayed with her for wisdom and obedience. Then she surprised Lela. "I'll be glad to help hold you accountable, Lela. But what you and your young man need is couple's counseling."

"But we're not even engaged. We both feel God has put us together, and I *hope* he's the man I'm going to marry. But I don't know that yet."

"I understand. However; you and Henry obviously consider yourself a couple. And, as you've just said, engaged or not, marriage isn't far from your mind. Have you two talked marriage?"

"Yes." Lela smiled. "I know that's what we both want. Henry is a good bit older than I, but he isn't pushing me. In fact, I guess we're both trying not to push each other. We've not known each other a terribly long time."

It was Jean's turn to smile, her brown eyes radiating amusement. "That doesn't always matter. I'm not saying it shouldn't matter for you two, but my husband and I dated for three months and knew we didn't need to wait any longer. As soon as we could plan a small wedding we were married. That was four children and thirty-five years ago, so I think it's going to last."

Lela laughed. "I would hope so! Actually, that makes me feel better. I know I'm not ready to walk down the aisle yet, but I'm not sure I want to wait for a long time either. Marrying Henry and having children with him sounds so good to me." She looked at Jean with a more serious attitude. "I guess you'll tell me God being the center of the relationship is what really matters?"

"Absolutely. That's why I want you to have counseling. A pastor who is well trained can be invaluable to a young couple, even if you decided you weren't meant to marry one another. In fact, that might be what you decide, after counseling." Jean leaned forward in her chair. "But more than likely, it will help you both to see how to be better to one another, how to grow in your faith together, and what marriage really is; and how to have the best one you can."

"I want that." Lela said softly. "Henry is the kindest person, and I would always want to be my best for him. He's so good to me, and I'd never want to hurt him or make mistakes that could be avoided."

"Good for you. And it looks to me as though Henry would be blessed to have you for a helpmate. Why don't you talk this over with Henry? If you need some names, I know a few pastors who are excellent counselors. Our own pastor is one of them."

"Thank you. Yes, let me talk to Henry. I can't imagine why he'd object. He might even know of someone he'd like to counsel us."

They said their good-byes, and as soon as Lela got home, she dialed Henry's cell phone. Leaving a message, she wandered into the kitchen to snack on the salad her mother was preparing for supper. As Lela told her mother what Jean had said, her mother nodded in agreement.

"I wish there had been more of that when your daddy and I got married. The first year was rough because we didn't know *how* to be married. We struggled with having our own way and getting our feelings hurt and being immature in general. I imagine a lot of that could have been avoided if we'd been counseled first."

"Maybe that's why a lot of marriages don't make it."

"Maybe so. But we both loved God and as Christians, had no plans to end the marriage. We simply had to pray and feel our way through some difficult times. There's no point in anyone causing hardship for one another when it isn't necessary." She wiped her hands on the towel and put the salad in the refrigerator. "Don't get the wrong impression, though. No matter how much counseling you get, and no matter how much you and Henry may love one another and think you know one another, if you get married, there will still be surprises and misunderstandings that you can't possibly foresee. Just know they're coming and be willing to work through them."

"Thanks, Mama." Lela looked at her mother fondly. "I'm glad we can talk. I know Emmie and her mom have trouble sometimes and she feels like her mother doesn't understand her."

"*Always* feel free to talk to me. You and I can work through things too, you know." She turned toward the stove. "Now, set the table and I'll get the bread in the oven. Your daddy should be home any minute and I'd like us to sit down together for a change."

The phone rang just as her mother finished her sentence. Lela grabbed the cordless and saw from caller I.D. it was Henry calling her back. "Hey!"

"Hey Lela, what's up?"

"Well, I've got about five minutes before supper. Can you talk?"

"Sure."

Lela explained to Henry what Jean Smithfield had shared with her.

"Makes sense to me. Anything to help us grow and learn."

"Do you want to use my pastor or someone else she recommends?"

"How would you feel about my pastor?" Henry asked. "Your town is so small. To be honest, I'm afraid people would see me and then rumors would start. My church is small, but my town is a whole lot bigger, providing less of a chance for gossip. Besides, they're used to seeing me around. I know my pastor has training as a counselor; I've got a buddy who went through pre-marital counseling with Pastor James a few years ago. He says it really helped them."

"That's fine with me. Will you call him?"

"I'll try to get hold of him tomorrow."

Lela's mother stuck her head around the corner and said, "Your daddy just pulled in."

"Daddy's here and supper is ready, so I better go. I miss you."

"I miss you too. I got all excited when I saw it was you who called. I wanted to tell you I got the concert tickets for you and Emmie. You are finally gonna to hear me on stage."

"Emmie will flip! I can't wait to tell her. I've been keeping it a surprise."

Henry sighed. "I need to go too. I promised some friends I'd jam with them like we used to. I'll call you tomorrow when we can really talk."

"Sounds good. Take care, Henry."

"You too,darlin'. I think I love you, Lela."

"I think I love you, Henry. Bye."

She hung up smiling and went to greet her father.

The houselights dimmed. Emmie squeezed Lela's arm so tightly she flinched. The concert hall was sold out, but as the lights went down, the huge crowd became silent.

Two chords from the guitar and Henry's voice suddenly came from everywhere. The crowd went crazy as people stood, looking for him in all directions. One by one, spotlights popped on, revealing band members and back up singers. But Henry was nowhere to be seen. Lela had an adrenalin rush as she felt the crowd's energy building to a frenzy before Henry finally appeared above the band on a catwalk that had been hidden in the shadowy rafters. For a few seconds neither Henry nor the band could be heard for the roar of the crowd. They settled slowly and in the quietness Henry's voice soared over all the music, making goose bumps stand out on Lela's arms. As the first song finished, the crowd was roaring again, everyone on their feet.

For the next two hours, Henry sang, talked, joked and interacted with the audience in a way that stunned Lela. What she saw, heard and felt wasn't Henry.

Up there on stage, he was *Hank* Fields, all the way.

Backstage the frenzy continued. Lela stood with Emmie, hand over her belly, feeling dazed and exhausted. From stagehands to VIP's, every inch was alive with activity. Henry was absent from the laughing crowd. Ted appeared, smiling. "Hello, ladies. How'd you like the concert?"

Emmie was bouncing. "It was absolutely the best fun I've ever had!" She turned to Lela. "Wasn't it great?"

"Yeah." Emmie and Ted both looked at her quizzically.

"Are you okay, Lela?" Emmie asked, peering at her closely.

"I'm fine. Just a little tired, I guess."

Ted took Lela firmly by the arm. "This may have been too much for you. Come on girls. I've got strict orders from the boss to get you back to his dressing room as quickly as possible. This way." They left the immediate back stage area and walked down a fairly narrow hallway until it opened up to a large open space. There were closed doors everywhere. From behind some of them you could hear laughter and smell food. Ted approached one of the doors and knocked.

Lela heard Henry's voice. "Come in."

When Henry saw Lela, he broke into a huge grin. It faltered quickly when he saw the look on her face. "Lela, what's wrong?"

"I guess I'm just tired." She mentally shook herself and smiled up at Henry. "You were great. I didn't realize what a performer you are."

He looked at her uncertainly. "Thanks. The crowd was really responsive tonight, that always makes me a better performer." He turned to Emmie. "I know who you are. I can't believe I've not met Lela's best friend till now."

He stuck out his hand, which Emmie shook enthusiastically. "It's nice meeting you, Hank. I was telling them it's the best time I've ever had. You have a fantastic voice."

"Please, call me Henry. Hank is for Ted and people who don't know me. And I suspect, since you're tight with Lela, we'll get to know each other soon." Then he turned back to Lela. "Do you need to sit down? You're worryin' me, here."

"I'm fine, really. I-I don't know what's wrong with me. But maybe we need to get on the road."

"Sure." Henry glanced up. "Ted, will you have the car brought around for them?"

"Of course. I'll be right back."

Emmie looked uncomfortable. She asked for a restroom, as though searching for an excuse to leave Henry and Lela alone. Henry showed her the way, and when he returned, he took Lela in his arms. "What is wrong?"

Lela's voice was muffled as she talked with her head buried in his chest. "I don't know." Then she burst into tears. Henry closed his eyes, capped his hand over the top of her head and held her.

Emmie came back in, saw the situation and backed slowly out. Ted did the same thing a few moments later. They stood out in the hall together. Ted asked, "Have they had a fuss or something?"

"No. She was all excited before the concert and they talked on the phone just minutes before we parked. Maybe she's just in pain. I don't have a clue, and usually I know her as well as I know myself."

"I guess we'll just stand here a few minutes. Let's pray while we're at it."

Back in the room, Lela finally pulled herself away from Henry. "I'm so sorry. I'm ruining everything."

Henry reached for a tissue and handed it to Lela to wipe her eyes and nose. "You're not ruining anything. I'm just concerned. Are you in pain, or has something upset you?"

"Well, I *feel* upset, but I don't know why. I think I just want to go home."

"Maybe it's all just been too much for you." He tilted her face toward his. "I'm off for two nights before we fly north to continue the tour. Maybe I can drive up tomorrow afternoon and we can spend a few hours together. How does that sound?"

"Maybe so. Call me tomorrow?"

"You know I will. Are you sure you're not upset with me?"

"You've done nothing to make me upset."

"Promise?"

"I promise."

"I love you, Lela. Let's get you home." She smiled weakly at him and nodded. He kissed her on the forehead. Opening the door, he found Ted and Emmie standing there, awkwardly waiting. He hugged Lela one more time, nodded to Emmie, looked helplessly at Ted and watched them walk out of sight. He raked his hand through his hair before stepping back into his dressing room and closing the door.

Emmie and Lela climbed into the back of the car awaiting them. As soon as they moved into traffic and settled onto the interstate headed toward home, Emmie turned to Lela. "Okay, spill. What the heck is the matter with you?"

Lela started crying again. "Something just happened to me. I know it sounds stupid, but it hit me for the first time that Henry is *famous*. It's like I don't know who he really is."

Emmie sighed. "I guess seeing him up there on stage brought it home to you, huh?"

"In a big way. We've known each other for months, but his fame has only been in the background to me. Almost like a game we were playing. I mean, I have his CD's, and I've even seen him on television a little bit, but to see him up there, bigger than life – and the way the crowd was screaming for him, it was like he wasn't my Henry anymore."

"But that doesn't really change who he is, Lela."

"Doesn't it? I think I've fooled myself into believing he's just an ordinary guy who can give me an ordinary life. That's not true." She shook her head. "It's not true at all." She turned to Emmie. "I don't know if I can handle all this. If I've fooled myself about something this big, what else am I not looking at?"

"Well, aren't you and Hank – Henry, I mean – in couples counseling?"

"Yes. We've been twice. I thought it went really well. Henry's pastor has talked about a lot of Biblical concepts regarding relationships and marriage. I've learned a lot. But you know what the funny thing is? We've never even mentioned Henry's lifestyle. It never entered my mind. I don't know if Pastor James doesn't get it either, or if he thought we had that worked out. And Henry hasn't talked about it in counseling at all." She laid her head back on the seat. "Henry tried to talk to me about it in the beginning, at least the downside part of fame. Rumors, and possibly being separated because of his travel, stuff like that. But I was confident that those things wouldn't be a problem. Now I don't even know if I can handle the *upside* to it."

"What are you saying?"

"I'm saying I don't know what I want anymore. I just need to go home and sleep."

"I think you need to go home and *pray*. Then you need to sit down with Henry and the pastor and work through this." Emmie tucked her foot under her. "Lela, I've spent weeks watching you glow every time Henry's name is even mentioned. Nothing you've said makes me think Henry Fields is anyone other than the guy he has shown to you. You may not have realized his charisma or power on stage, or even the extent of his talent, but doesn't that just make him more of who he is? If fame was going to change him, wouldn't it have changed him long before he met you?"

"I don't know. It's like thinking you know someone and you don't. I mean, what if you found out tomorrow that I had been secretly painting masterpieces all my life and you didn't know it and had never seen one, and suddenly they're everywhere and I'm famous for it? Wouldn't you feel duped or at least suspicious of me?"

"Sure. But Henry hasn't duped you at all. You've known almost from the get go he was famous. It's not his fault you didn't get to experience it from the beginning, or that you're just now seeing him in person on stage. In fact, from what you've told me, he's been very careful to hide absolutely nothing from you. Right?"

"I guess. I still feel tricked."

"Then I think you need to deal with the one who tricked you."

Lela looked up at Emmie, surprised. "And who would that be, exactly?"

"Look in the mirror, Lela. That would be you."

Henry stood leaned up against the door. He kept fighting back nausea, hoping he was going to be able to keep down what little food he had in his stomach. He had gone from being incredibly pumped to scared witless in a matter of moments. *'What's wrong, Lord, what's wrong with Lela?'* He had seen her in physical pain, he'd seen her angry and unsure. But he'd never seen this. He wracked his brain trying to think of something, anything that would explain her behavior. He came up empty. The quick conversation they'd had just before she'd arrived in the theatre had been full of excitement and happiness. He had known where she was sitting, of course, and had seen her during the concert off and on, but they had agreed not to call attention to her presence in the audience for security reasons. Only once had he allowed himself to truly focus in Lela's direction, and that had been when he had sung '*Falling*', his signature ballad that had propelled him to superstardom two years before. He sang to Lela because now that song described his present state to perfection. He was, indeed, falling. While on stage, he had felt nothing but elation and the joy of performing.

He walked over to the make up table and picked up his cell phone. He started dialing Lela's number, but stopped. He changed and called Ted instead. "I'm on my way, buddy." Ted responded.

"Do you know what's wrong?"

"Not a clue. Sorry."

"I hoped she'd say something."

"Her friend tried to make small talk on the way to the car, but Lela wasn't responding much."

"Oh. Well, I'll be ready to go in a few minutes."

"I'll be there. And Hank?"

"Yeah?"

"It'll be fine. God's large and in charge."

"Right." Henry closed the phone. "Come on, God, *please.. .*"

Lela's mother sat beside her on the bed, a bewildered look on her face. "Lela, I don't know what to say."

"I don't want to talk to him if he calls tonight. I'm confused and I know I'll upset him more if I talk to him."

"I disagree. You think by refusing to talk it's going to make him feel better? Silence is terrifying! Have you ever wanted God to answer you and instead you heard nothing? That's not fair, Lela."

"I'm not shooting for fair, Mama. I just want to be left alone for a few hours. *You* talk to him."

Her mother's eyes flashed. "I think I will. And I may start by apologizing for my daughter acting like a brat instead of an adult."

She stood. "Perhaps it's best he see this side of you now. After all, he deserves the right to change his mind too."

She walked out and closed the door. Lela turned, muffling her sobs in her pillow. Her mother stood on the other side of the door, shaking her head. Lela had listened to no one, Henry included, when they had talked to her about fame. She had been smug and confident that it was no big deal. Getting a taste of what that really meant this early in the relationship could be an opportunity for growth, if Lela was mature enough to handle it. Her mother had truly believed Lela had that level of maturity, until now. Now, well, she had to wonder.

She went into the den and spoke with Lela's father. They both agreed Henry deserved a phone call.

He picked up on the first ring. "Lela?"

"No, Henry. It's Vicki. Lela is in bed."

"Is she all right? Have I done something wrong?"

Voice soft, Lela's mother responded. "Not a thing. But I believe I know what's wrong *with* her."

"Please tell me. I've been crazy with worry."

"I knew you would be. That's why Art and I agreed I should call you." She paused, looking for the right words. "Lela is young, but we forget that sometimes because she's so mature in many ways. I think tonight really shook her up."

"Why? Was someone rude to her? Did someone frighten her? If so, you can bet there will be consequences-"

"No, no, it's nothing like that. She saw you on stage for the first time. She was among thousands of people who adore you. She saw their faces, heard their cheers, felt that adoration. I think it frightened her. For the first time, I believe, she understands that you really *are* famous, that you really *are* a star. It's not just make-believe. And if she becomes your wife someday, she's going to have to live with that. She's going to have to live with the fact that thousands of girls would change places with her in a second. That brings trusting you to a whole new level."

"Those girls mean nothing to me. It's almost as though they are an illusion. Even before I met Lela, it never entered my mind to answer a note, or take anyone up on an offer."

"But the notes come and the offers are there, aren't they?"

"Well, yes, but- "

"I don't think Lela really believed it before tonight."

Henry was silent for a moment. "So, what am I supposed to do? I can't change any of that. I'd give it up in a heartbeat for Lela, if I could. I love her, Mrs. Sawyer. I can't change that either. Tell me what to do."

"Just sit tight. Leave her alone for tonight. Call your pastor tomorrow and set up an appointment, if you can, before you have to leave for tour. If he can see ya'll, we'll make sure Lela gets there. She needs to be confronted about her fears and she needs to face you and talk about them. Hiding won't solve anything and we're not going to let her do that. If she decides she can't take it after she meets with you and the pastor, well, then, I guess we'll go from there, won't we?"

"I don't think I can stand it, if that's what happens."

"Henry, God can see any of us through the very worst. You believe that, don't you?"

"In theory, anyway."

"Son, you better believe it in all ways. It's the truth. Faith isn't much use in theory."

"I know." He sighed heavily. "I'm gonna try and get some sleep. I'll contact Pastor James first thing in the mornin'. I'll call you as soon as I know what time we can be seen. If I have to cancel my next concert, so be it. I can't take this."

"Careful, Henry. Pray about this. I don't know that canceling is the right thing to do. At any rate, maybe that won't be a problem. We'll be praying too. Meanwhile, I'll try to refrain from marching into Lela's room and giving her a good spanking." She heard Henry chuckle. "We love you Henry. Have faith!"

"Thanks." Henry choked up. "I really am countin' on you being my in-laws. Pray hard."

They hung up and Henry found himself on his knees, asking for guidance and wisdom.

Chapter Ten

*H*enry's heart twisted as he watched Lela step out of her parent's car. She straightened and looked fearfully back at the car as she slammed the door. He couldn't see who had driven her, but the car pulled away from the curb, leaving Lela standing there, looking as though she might bolt after it. When the car was out of sight, she dropped her head for a moment, then headed for the church. Henry hoped the dropped head was in prayer.

He'd done a ton of praying himself in the last twenty-four hours. He'd resisted the desire to call her a dozen times, knowing that Pastor James had agreed to see them quickly. It had been the longest time of his life, however; no matter how quickly the appointment had been set up.

As she opened the church doors, she saw him standing there, and she hesitated. He watched her eyes brighten with unshed tears as she walked toward him. "Hey Henry." She searched his face. "Are you okay?"

He willed his hands to stay at his sides, instead of touching her as they longed to do. "Yeah." Could she be any more beautiful to him? "I've been worried about you, Lela."

She closed her eyes. "I'm so sorry about all this. I don't know what's wrong with me." She looked at him. "But I want you to know

I'm through with being a big baby. I've been praying and God has convicted me of that, at least."

Henry smiled at her. "I don't pretend to know what's wrong, but I'm glad you've been praying about it. Prayer is the only thing that's kept *me* going." They both turned as the office door opened behind them.

It was Pastor James. His ruddy complexion stood out against the white knit shirt he wore and his dark hair was just long enough to touch its collar. "Well, I see you're both here. Come on in and have a seat. I've got to check one thing, then I'll join you."

Henry followed Lela into the pastor's office and closed the door. They sat silently until Pastor James came back into the dark paneled room and settled himself behind the desk. "Let's start off with prayer, shall we?" They bowed their heads. "Father God, we come to You today to ask for guidance in the lives of these two young people. They both love You, Lord and want Your will to be done in their lives. Give me wisdom to assist them in this endeavor. Remove any hindrances that might be in this room that would stop them from obedience. In the name of Your Son and Our Beloved Savior, Jesus Christ, Amen." He looked up at both of them and smiled. "Now, I hear there's been a bump in the road. Want to tell me what happened?"

Henry glanced at Lela. She looked up from examining her hands, lower lip trembling. "I don't know where to start."

Pastor James leaned forward in his chair. "Tell me when you started getting upset."

Lela took a deep breath. "My best friend, Emmie and I went to Henry's concert. It was the first time ever for me to see him perform, and she and I were both so excited. But when Henry came out on stage, and everyone started screaming – I don't know – I began to feel so afraid! All the people, girls mostly, are obviously so devoted to him, it's almost scary." She paused for a moment, as though remembering. "And then I looked at Henry." Her voice dropped to a whisper. "It didn't even *look* like him. He suddenly looked bigger than life and so powerful and confident and sexy." Color suffused her cheeks. "Sorry. But suddenly I felt very insignificant and lost." She looked up at Pastor James, careful not to glance Henry's way. "I realized I'm no match for that guy up on stage. He doesn't need me in any way, and I can't imagine what he'd ever see in me, or why he'd ever want me." She dropped her head. "Or how he could ever love me."

Henry sat dumbfounded. He looked at Pastor James, who just raised his eyebrows at him. Henry turned to Lela. "Are you kiddin' me? That guy on stage is *me* Lela. Me, just doin' my job. The only difference I feel is the rush, the pleasure it gives me, to be up there. It doesn't change who I am, it's just something I *do*. When I walked off that stage, the only person I was thinkin' of was you. I couldn't wait to see you. I couldn't wait to hear how you thought it went." It was Henry's turn to lower his voice. "I couldn't wait to hear you say you thought I did good."

"And instead I acted all upset."

"Instead you couldn't wait to leave. You couldn't wait to get away from me."

"Because I was scared. I was scared *sick*. I thought I was going to throw up." She finally looked at Henry. "Who am I kidding, Henry? You're a superstar. Not just a guy I met, not somebody who leads a normal life like me. You're in a different league."

"Do you want me to give it up? Will that make me acceptable in your eyes?" For the first time, Henry began to get angry. "I've made a very concentrated effort to stay away from all the Hollywood hoopla. Not because I was afraid I'd be tempted to change, but because it's nothing I'm interested in. I've never been dishonest with you, Lela. I am who I say I am. What you see is what you get. But now I wonder if that's true with you."

"*Me?*" Lela looked astounded. "You know who I am. No glitter here."

"And where is all the glitter you see about me? On stage? What did I do on stage that is contrary to anything I've ever told you?"

"Well, nothing, exactly, but-"

"But, what?"

She threw her hands up. "I don't know! It made me feel like I didn't know who you were."

Henry turned his glare on the pastor. "A little help here?"

Pastor James looked startled. "Huh? Oh." He looked caught off guard. "Boy, you two sure do put on a good fight." He turned to Lela. "Sounds like you had a little culture shock." He smiled at Henry. "I saw you in concert not too long ago. I know exactly what Lela is talking about in regards to how you look up there. Half the night I kept asking myself, *'is that really Henry Fields up there?'* Of course, I didn't feel like I had anything to lose, so I simply sat back in disbelief and enjoyed the show."

Henry ran his hands through his hair. "I honestly don't know what ya'll are talkin' about."

They both looked at him in amazement. "Henry, it's called charisma. And you have it by the boatloads." Pastor James continued. "Don't get me wrong, you're a likable fella on a daily basis. But it looks like a magical transformation takes place when you step out on that stage. You do look taller and powerful and confident and in charge. Sexy." He grinned. "Impressed me."

Henry shook his head. "Okay. Whatever. But why has that caused so much bad stuff to go on inside you?" He asked Lela. "It seems to me it would make you proud of me and pleased that I could provide for our family." He snorted. "If that's even a possibility anymore. I feel like you're about to throw me out on my ear."

Before Lela could rise to the bait, Pastor James asked Henry, "Out of curiosity, may I ask why Lela has never attended any previous performance?"

"Timing, I guess. I was finishing up a tour when I first met her, then I was off tour for several weeks with other projects."

"So there wasn't an opportunity for her to see you perform anywhere? Not even informal jam sessions?"

" Well, I guess she could have come to something-"

"You never invited me. You've never invited me to your house either. Just out – out to eat, out to Disney World, out with your parents. But never to meet friends or watch you sing."

Pastor James cocked his head. "Hmm. Why is that Henry?"

Henry sat very still. He had a blank look on his face, then puzzlement. He seemed to really be thinking about what had been asked. "How weird." He muttered to himself. "I don't know. It's never been a conscious thing." He looked at Lela. "I don't have much time to spend with old friends, and I guess I never thought about linking you up with them yet. They know about you, though. I get constant ribbing about how much I talk about you and about how young you are."

"Anything else? Like why not invite her to your house instead of out with your parents?"

"I guess I was afraid she wouldn't like the house. And what if she didn't? I spent a lot of money on it. What if we do get married and she hates the house? Man, I really love that house."

"Oh, for pete's sake, Henry. Why would I hate the house? And besides, even if it wasn't what I'd prefer, I'd never make you sell something you loved."

"I know. But I wouldn't be happy in it anymore, if you weren't happy in it. I guess I was putting it off in case you did hate it."

Lela rolled her eyes but stayed silent, arms crossed against her chest.

"What about the no invites to jam sessions or small performances?" Pastor James asked.

Henry sighed. "I think I already know the answer to that. It's been in the back of my mind for a while." He leaned forward in his chair and tilted it so he was closer to Lela. "You have given me such joy and seemed to have enjoyed being with me. And it had nothing to do with what I did for a living. You have no idea how careful I've had to be in letting new people into my life. I am always having to ask: What do they want? Do they really like me, or like what I can do for them or their careers? I liked having you separated from my job." Henry suddenly seemed to find his hands fascinating. "I remember how happy I was that you didn't act differently towards me when you found out I was famous. I think I was terrified that you'd act differently when you *saw* I was famous. And you have." He let out a short laugh. "Not exactly in the way I was worried about, but boy, you sure have acted differently."

"Perhaps that's why Lela feels the way she does. Perhaps she realized how left out she's been and wonders why. *Perhaps* that's why she felt 'insignificant and lost'."

"Oh, Lord, Lela, if that's so, I'm sorry." Henry gave in and grasped her hands. "Please forgive me if I've hurt you." He looked pleadingly into her eyes. "I may not be very good at this relationship stuff. But I do love you. And I want to get better at this. I want to learn how to be selfless instead of selfish." He let go of her hands to once again rake through his hair. "I guess first I have to learn how to realize *when* I'm being selfish."

Lela felt fresh tears starting. "Maybe that *is* why I've been feeling this way. I thought it was my inadequacies alone. I've never had boyfriends much and don't know what to expect all the time. I figured you needed time with your buddies without me horning in. I also thought I'd be in your way at practices." She paused for a moment. "Then when I watched you on stage, and went backstage afterwards and realized I didn't know one single person there except Ted, I saw how much of your life I wasn't a part of. I knew I couldn't settle being a little part of your life. And I wasn't sure if or how I could fit in to the rest of it. I decided if you didn't think I was a good fit, then I wasn't."

"Man, is there anything I *haven't* messed up?" Henry asked, looking heavenward. "Is there anything I can do to fix this, make it right?" He asked Lela.

She shrugged. "Do you really love me, or love the idea of having someone love you?"

"Oh, that one I can answer without a doubt. I love you. You know, I can imagine my life without ever going on stage again. I can even imagine my life without ever singing again, although I'd miss being able to sing. But I've tried these past hours to imagine my life without you, and I can't. Or at least it scares me so much I don't want to try."

Lela looked at Pastor James. "How do we go on from here? How do we fix this mess?"

"Well, Lela, first of all, do you *want* to go on from here with Henry?"

She smiled faintly. "Part of me wants to say no. I think I'm angrier than I realized for feeling so left out. But I think that would be cutting my nose off to spite my face." She turned to Henry. "If we do go on from here, I don't want to be left out. I'm not saying I have to be with you twenty-four/seven, but I don't want to feel like I'm being purposefully left out of something because you selfishly want to keep things separate."

"I won't make that mistake again, Lela. But I can't promise you I won't make others." He frowned. "Maybe I'm no good at this. Maybe that's why I'm pushing thirty and you're the first serious relationship I've ever had."

"I don't expect you to be perfect. I shouldn't have kept this bottled up inside, either. I won't do that again, but I'm sure I'll make other mistakes too. I just don't want us to keep making the same ones over."

"Neither do I."

Pastor James spoke up. "Then it's settled. We will go on from here. I suggest you both take this time to apologize to one another and then we will pray and ask God to heal and help us move on."

Henry once again clasped Lela's hands. "I am so sorry for excluding you and being selfish. Will you please forgive me?"

"Yes, I forgive you, Henry. And I am sorry for not talking things out with you and letting you know I was feeling left out. Will you forgive me?"

"You are forgiven, darlin'."

They bowed in prayer. "Father God, thank you for this time together. Only You know our true hearts. Please provide healing for Henry and Lela and allow them to move forward from these mistakes without ever looking back on them or holding onto the feelings attached to them. Help them turn loose of that right now. Thank you Lord. Show us how to proceed and grow this relationship in the way You would have it grow. In Jesus' precious name, amen."

Lela and Henry stood up and embraced. With one arm still around Lela's shoulders, Henry turned to Pastor James to shake his hand. "Thank you so much, sir. I want you to know how grateful I am to you. I don't know if we could get through all this without your guidance."

"That's what I'm here for, Henry. You two have a little bit more to deal with than most couples, in a way. But in other ways, you are far beyond some of the pitfalls I see. The most important part of all this is for you two to pray for one another and with one another. Do some Bible study together, too. If you can arrange it, worship together occasionally. Learn how to serve God as a couple. Doing this will show you God's intentions about marriage."

As they walked outside, Lela's father drove up. She turned to Henry. "I still feel a little awkward."

"I know. Me too. May I call you tonight?"

"You better!" They both smiled, easing the tension a bit.

"I hate that I've got to fly off tomorrow. But we'll keep in touch until I'm closer home again." He put his hands on her shoulders. "Lela, I'm not gonna live like this forever. In a few years my contract will be up, and I can negotiate however I want. I can quit altogether, if necessary. Please believe me when I say I want whatever God wants in my life. And I believe He's placed you in it. I'll never shortchange that again. I'd never be gone all the time leaving you or our kids, either."

Lela searched his face. "I know you always do your best. I believe you, Henry. I want what He wants too." She smiled. "Call me tonight. We'll talk more. You'll be home again before we know it and we'll map out this relationship thing together."

"That sounds like the best news I've heard lately." He hugged her close, mindful that her father was not two feet away. "I can't kiss you with your daddy right there." Lela laughed. "Then I'll kiss you." She tiptoed and planted a quick one on his lips, opened the door and climbed in. "I'll be waiting on your call. About eight?"

"About eight." She closed the door and as Lela's dad waved to Henry, they drove away.

Chapter Eleven

s Henry's absence grew, the long distance conversations turned more and more to marriage. And *'if* we get married' turned into *'when* we get married'. Neither of them acknowledged the change as it occurred, nor did they talk about it as they rode to his parent's house for Lela to stay the night so she could go to church with them the next morning.

They sat around after supper, talking and looking at photos and videos of Henry and his family. Lela began to get a real sense of that family and how they interacted. She felt the sweet spirit that permeated their home, and it filled her with a peace and confidence about their future together.

"Oh, look at this picture!" Henry's mother exclaimed. It was Henry at about a year, looking up from the tub, suds on his nose.

Lela giggled. "Lord, Henry. Our kids will never stand a chance. Their hair will be so curly we'll never know which end of the corkscrew to cut."

He studied the top of her head. "Your hair ain't all that curly."

"Is too. I just use big rollers and straighten it some."

"You use rollers to *straighten* your hair?"

"Yes, and it works. You should try it sometime." She said smugly. Lela turned to his mother. "Will you make sure photographs are taken of that too?"

"Oh, absolutely, dear." She smiled at her son. "Tabloids are always looking for new stuff."

"At least it would be real. No! Wait! There's no way the famous Hank Fields would straighten his beautiful, naturally curly locks."

They all threw popcorn at him. Henry's father admonished him, saying, "Son, you ain't too big to still take a trip to the woodshed if your head gets too fat, with or without rollers."

Lela and Henry sat out on the front porch, putting off the time coming for him to drive the short distance to his own house for the night. They were rocking in tandem, holding hands between the chairs. Honeysuckle and jasmine perfume hung heavy in the evening air, as the tree frogs tuned up to begin their night serenade. "I'm sorry I missed your birthday." Henry said softly. "I bought you a present, but lost it on the plane."

"This is present enough. Turning nineteen is a pretty big deal, though. My last year as one of those teens you fear so much."

"Very funny. Just for that I won't be replacin' that expensive gift I lost."

"Uh huh. Seriously, Henry, calling me in the middle of the concert and singing happy birthday to me on a borrowed cell phone from an audience member was spending enough money. Oh, my bad. That didn't cost you anything, did it?"

"Except maybe a fan." He grinned in the dark. "Course, she was singin' too. Heck, they were all singin' to you. When I told them I finally had a girlfriend, they laughed. Then when they realized I was serious, I got – or maybe you got – a standin' ovation. It was way cool."

"Did you tell them how old I was?"

"No way. I no longer think it's a good idea to talk about your age. Your eyes get all squinty and mean lookin' if I do." He shuddered in mock fear.

Changing the subject abruptly, Lela blurted, 'I'm nervous about church tomorrow.'

Henry looked surprised. "Why? They won't ask your age."

"Ha, ha. I don't know anyone there, and I want them to think you've made a good choice."

"Lela, they won't look at you with their eyes as much as they'll look at you with their hearts. When they do that, they'll know I've made a good choice."

"Thanks, Henry. Make sure to sit close."

He squirmed uncomfortably in the rocker. "Well, I won't be sittin' with you at first. I generally sing in the choir when I'm home, but we'll come down to the congregation after the choir special. I asked a couple of my friends to sit in the same pew as us, so you won't feel all alone. But if you really want me to, I'll not sing and sit with you the whole service."

"Oh, no. The choir never entered my mind." Lela chuckled. "You'd think it would have. I'll be fine as long as I can see you."

"Are you sure?"

"Absolutely."

"I hope you like my church. I want us to both be sure about the church we attend and be satisfied. I was raised in that church, and I want our kids to be happy like I've always been. But I'm willing to try other places if you want."

"Agreed." Lela looked up at Henry. "Does it seem strange to you we're talking about our future like this? I guess I should feel weird about it, but it feels so good to me."

"It makes me happy. To think that I get to spend the rest of my life with you fills me with so much joy, Lela. I thank God for it all the time."

"Me too. I want to be the best wife someday. I'm glad we found each other."

"Oh, yeah, I almost forgot to mention I've got a little surprise for you tomorrow."

Lela narrowed her eyes suspiciously. "Like what?"

"Maybe you didn't hear me. I said '*surprise*' as in if I tell you, it won't be."

"I'm not sure I like surprises."

"What a shame."

"Well, will I like this one?"

"I hope so." They rocked some more. "There's another very important person in my life I want you to meet soon."

"Who would that be?" Lela asked.

"My grandfather. Growing up an only child I was doted on by every adult in my life. He's the only grandparent I have left. We're very close. He's the person who taught me to love music and embrace it no matter if other kids called me sissy or lame."

"All my grandparents are gone now. I never knew my mother's father, he was killed in service. Her mother died in a car wreck just before I was born. Daddy's parents both died fairly young too. I always envied Emmie because she had all these older adults hopelessly in love with her."

"It does seem like grandparents love you in a different way than parents. Gramms has been gone for several years. Papa has carried on alone, though. I know he misses her. He talks about her all the time. Maybe when I get back into town we can ride up and you can meet him. Let me warn you, he's very country. A true Appalachian."

"If he spoils me, I don't care how country he is."

Henry grinned. "I'll make sure he knows it." He looked at her. "Isn't it odd we're both only children? None of my friends were."

"Only one girl I knew was. Mama and Daddy didn't have more because they were both raised pretty poor and decided they only wanted one so they could afford whatever I needed."

"My mother got sick and had to have surgery right after I was born, so they never had more. But I had a cousin I was tight with and lots of friends as I grew older, so I don't figure I've missed too much."

"I've got cousins too, one the very same age. We've always had each other at family reunions and stuff. It's not too bad. But I do want to make sure we have more than one."

"Yeah, me too. I want at least a dozen."

"So you've said. I hope modern science can figure out a way for you to do that."

Henry grabbed his belly and groaned. "Okay, two or three will be plenty."

"That's better." She pulled his hand to her mouth and kissed the knuckles.

He squeezed her hand and stood up. "I better get goin' so I can be up bright and early for church." As Lela stood up, Henry put his arms around her and pulled her close. "I missed you so much. Every time we're apart, it gets worse."

"For me too."

He bent and kissed her. He marveled again at how much and how strongly he cared. "Good night. I think I love you, Lela."

"Good night, Henry. I think I love you too." He touched her cheek with his hand, and with a wave, he was gone.

As Lela was getting ready for bed, she heard a light tapping on her door, followed by a "Good night honey," from Henry's mother. Lela quickly opened the door.

"Thank you so much for having me. I've really enjoyed tonight."

"We've enjoyed it too." She smiled. "Henry's one blessed young man to find you. Don't let him forget it, either." She winked at Lela before going on down the hall to bed.

Lela closed the door again, picked up her cell phone and called home. She and her mother chatted briefly before her mother asked, "How is your pain?"

Lela absently felt her belly. "It comes and goes. My lower back hurts some too. If it gets much worse, I want to check with the doctor one more time. I hate to say this, but I'm beginning to think they're annoyed with me. I feel like they believe I'm malingering, or something."

"Sometimes doctors aren't happy with the patient if the patient doesn't recuperate the way they think a patient should. Don't let that attitude keep you from seeking help, Lela. Listen to your intuition. God gives us that gift, and He means for us to use it, not ignore it. Why don't we set up a doctor appointment for next week? Just to be on the safe side."

Lela sighed. "I guess you're right. I do feel like there's more to all this than post-surgery or even post injury pain. I can't put my finger on it, and I'm not saying there's something seriously wrong, but something *is* wrong."

"That settles it, then. We'll call Monday for an appointment. So, are you excited about church in the morning?"

"A little nervous. But it'll be interesting to meet all the people Henry's gone to church with his whole life. He says he has a surprise for me afterwards. I'll call Daddy and let him know where to meet us Sunday night to pick me up. I hate for Henry to drive nearly two hours just to take me home when he's got to be on a plane by eleven Monday morning."

"Your daddy is fine with meeting you half way. Where's Henry off to now?"

"He's actually doing a music camp for kids. He'll be giving pointers in voice. At the end of the week, he's giving a free mini-concert for the whole camp. He's more excited about this than I've seen him be over a concert in front of thousands."

"Henry's a good boy, Lela. His heart is certainly in the right place. I believe you have a keeper."

"Yeah." Lela paused for a moment. "Mama, we've been talking more and more about getting married. And it seems like every where I turn, there's some cute curly headed little boy around reminding me how much I'd love to have babies that look like Henry."

"I hope you decide to wait a little while, though."

"We are. I just wanted you to know we are talking. No plans or anything, more like dreaming right now, I guess. I've got school to think about, and Henry's got all sorts of commitments too. But it sure is nice to dream with him."

"I know, honey. Just keep at least one foot on the ground."

"I promise I will. I'll see you tomorrow night. Tell Daddy I love him and good night."

Lela hung up the phone, grabbed her Bible out of her bag and read till she fell asleep.

Chapter Twelve

The church sat nestled in a wooded area, huge oaks protectively surrounding it. The white clapboard building looked freshly painted. The wide double doors were standing open in welcome. The steeple rose sharply, sunlight glinting off the tip of the cross that topped it.

Inside the church, heavy beams supported the lofty ceiling, and rainbows shot all over the sanctuary, formed by the stained glass windows that lined the outer walls. Behind the pulpit, a beautiful baptismal stood at the ready, with a massive, rugged cross hanging on the wall above it.

Lela sat nervously waiting. Henry had disappeared behind the doors to the left of the pulpit. She heard people laughing and talking all around her, but at this moment she felt oddly alone. She saw the door open and grinned as Henry flew toward her, choir robe billowing out behind him. "Sorry I was gone so long. Jordie and Jack's kids just puked all over the nursery and they had to go home. Mama and Daddy are in the choir room getting ready. Are you sure you don't want me to pull this thing off and sit with you instead of sing?"

"I'll be fine, Henry. I'm looking forward to seeing you up there." She nodded toward the choir loft. "I may wave or make faces."

"Don't tempt me, girl. I might just do the same." He raked his hand through his hair, which made it much worse than it already was. "As soon as the choir special is over, I'm coming down to sit with you." He patted her hand and flew back through the door.

"He's a mess, ain't he?" Lela looked up to find an elderly gentleman standing there, propped up on the back of the pew. He was grinning widely, and his eyes danced as he looked at her.

"Yes sir, he is." She stuck out her hand. "I'm Lela Sawyer, a friend of Henry's."

He gave her hand a firm grasp. "Don't I know it. I'm Asa Cummings, Henry's Papa. He's been talkin' to me about you, so I decided I'd show up this mornin' and worship with ya'll instead of my reg'lar church. Mind if I sit?" He motioned next to Lela.

"Not at all, please sit! You're Papa! This is great. Henry's mentioned you too. He tells me you taught him all about music."

"I reckon I learned him all I knowed. Ain't sayin' that was much, mind you." He settled into the pew. "He's a awful good boy, Henry is. From what he tells me, you're a good 'un. That right?"

"I hope so. I try to be, anyway."

"Do you love the Lord?"

"Yes sir, I do."

"All that matters, in the end. Love Him and serve Him and you'll do fine, good times and bad."

The pianist started playing softly as the choir entered. Henry lit up like a Christmas tree when he saw his papa. Lela watched as Henry's mother looked surprised, then did a little wave to her father.

When the choir special was over, Henry sat on the other side of Lela, draping his robed arm behind her.

The pastor made announcements and welcomed visitors, noting that "Henry seems to have done something extraordinarily good or extraordinarily bad to have his grandfather as well as his girlfriend supervising, I mean, visiting today." The congregation laughed.

As they struck up the last hymn, Lela felt Henry leaning towards her and realized he was trying to hear her sing. She looked up at him and shook her head, but he just grinned at her. She tried to sing very, very softly. Her face flushed. She hoped he hadn't heard a single note.

After church, Lela was greeted warmly by young and old alike. The older members each had a story to tell about Henry, usually dating back to when he was an incorrigible ten year old. Henry blushed and took it like a man.

After saying good-bye to his mother and father as well as Asa, who was being unwillingly dragged to a local restaurant, they climbed in Henry's car and headed toward his house. Henry teased her about her beautiful soprano and she threatened to sing to him in the car if he didn't shut up.

As they pulled into the driveway, Lela noticed a strange car parked over to the side of the garage. "Who's here?"

"Part of the surprise." He opened the car door for her. Lela stopped and stared at the house.

Henry had built in a farmhouse style. There was a long front porch, which carried on to the side of the house, where a portion of it had been screened it. They went in through there. "I love this house, Henry. How could you have thought I wouldn't?"

The door opened to the kitchen, where a tiny white-headed woman was cooking a large amount of food.

"Hey Sonja, we're here." She looked up and wiped her hands on a towel before shaking Lela's hand. "Sonja helps me so much. She cooks for me three or four days a week when I'm home and makes sure I don't sleep on dirty sheets or have dusty furniture."

"You sure are cooking a lot of food!" Lela exclaimed as she looked over the huge bowls of potatoes, beans, slaw and corn. There was a giant platter of piping hot fried chicken next to the stove and a basket full of golden biscuits, steam rising from under the warming towel.

"I cook whatever Henry tells me to. He eats like a pig, you know."

"I do not!" He affected a hurt look, which made the women laugh. Then he turned to Lela. "You and I are gonna eat *part* of this food. The rest of the surprise is some of my buddies are coming over in a little while for a jam session and I figured I'd better feed them too, so they'd keep being my friends." He looked down at Lela. "It's about time you meet all those close to me, don't you think?"

"I'm looking forward to it."

Sonja removed her apron and got ready to go. "Lemonade and tea are in the fridge. There are some soft drinks in there too. I gotta go and feed my own army." She turned to Lela. "It's nice meeting you, honey. Henry's a good boy. You take care of him now."

"That's what everyone tells me," Lela said with a smile. "I promise I'll be good to him."

Henry and Lela had just finished eating when they heard car doors slamming and people laughing. "They're here!" Henry exclaimed. He looked as excited as a twelve year old.

Lela stood and looked out the screen door. "Oh, my lord! What is *that*?"

"What?" Henry peered out over her head and grinned. "That, my dear, is Pistol."

At the sound of his name, the giant dog loped toward the door and woofed for Henry to open up. "Pistol, meet Lela. Lela, Pistol." Pistol sat and offered a giant paw. Lela shook it solemnly.

"Henry, I think I'm in love. What kind of dog are you, Pistol? Part elephant, maybe?"

His black masked bulldog face creased into a grin as he cocked his head at Lela, as though he knew exactly what she was saying.

"Pistol's mama was a Bull Mastiff and his daddy was half Old English Mastiff and half Great Dane. Thank God they were all fawn with black masks. But please don't talk about his weight! He's easily offended. He only weights a little over two hundred."

"Move that fat mutt out of the way so we can get in," groused a tall, dark, black- headed guy. "My wife is delicate and must be seated." Standing behind him was a very pregnant woman who had the bluest eyes Lela had ever seen.

As the screen door tapped Pistol's rear, he got up, wiggling all over. "Lela, this lovely couple is Seth and Sara Jones. They baby sit Pistol for me when I'm traveling."

Lela looked astounded. "You mean this is *your* dog?"

Seth and Sara cracked up. "Henry Fields, have you not told her about this monster?" Sara asked.

Henry looked sheepish. "Um, I forgot."

Seth shook his head sadly. "See what you've gotten yourself into, Lela? If I'd had your phone number, I would have warned you. But now, it's too late. Henry loves you. And whoever Henry loves, must stay."

Another car pulled up and Henry introduced John and Ashley, who had been dating for a year or so after being childhood friends, and Spenser, the last member of the band Henry had played with since high school. Spenser claimed to be the last confirmed bachelor, as he "had been hurt deeply by his only true love and could never love again."

At this proclamation, John looked up and said to Spenser, "Dude, that was seventh grade, you need to move on." The crowd hooted in delight, making Pistol bark enthusiastically.

If Lela had misgivings before meeting Henry's friends, they disappeared that afternoon. The two women made her feel as if she had been a part of the group forever. After everyone had eaten, the guys had gone downstairs to set up their instruments while the girls cleaned up the kitchen.

When they finished the dishes, they went downstairs to listen. Lela was impressed with the huge room Henry had designed for music. There was a giant screen T.V. and state of the art sound equipment. The seating was roomy and comfortable. To the side was a bar set up with a tiny microwave and refrigerator for snacks. As they enjoyed the music and on going comedy the guys provided, Lela got to know the girls and learned how they had all known Henry before his fame. They vowed he was the very same guy with a heart for Christ and a love for people. They regaled her with tales of their astonishment as they watched Henry become famous in an almost overnight fashion. Of all the people they had known, Henry had been the least likely to be spotlighted. He had always professed the desire to teach, and all admitted that better suited his rather dorky personality and looks. They said it all with fondness and a protectiveness that Lela found endearing.

As everyone left late that evening (except Pistol, who was spending the night before Henry had to fly out again tomorrow), Lela marveled at how much fun she had experienced in just one day.

Waving to the last of Henry's friends, they closed the door and stood in the kitchen, holding one another. Pistol lay on the floor with his side propped against the wall; all four giant paws dangling in mid-air. "Did you have fun?" Henry asked, kissing the top of Lela's head.

"Yeah. You do a pretty good job with those surprises."

"Thank you. They're a great bunch of friends." Henry unwrapped himself from her arms and walked over to the refrigerator, rooting around till he found a chicken leg to gnaw on. He raised his eyebrows in question, offering it to Lela. She shook her head no. "I've known them all but Seth my entire life. Seth moved here in seventh grade and started going to my church. We became instant friends. He was the only guy I knew who looked more like a nerd than me. The next year we started a band. Boy, we stunk too. Our parents used to try and pay each other off so practice wouldn't be held at their house."

"Well, you've improved a little since then."

"You're too kind," Henry said dryly. "I'll be sure and repeat the compliment next time I talk to them." He glanced at the kitchen clock. "I guess you need to call your daddy and let him know we're on our way." He laid the chicken down and took her in his arms again. "I hate for this day to end, but I've got a tough schedule next week, startin' tomorrow bright and early. I'm gonna to miss you, again." He bent down and kissed her, savoring the moment.

"Mmmmm."

Henry grinned down at her. "I'm a pretty good kisser, huh?"

Lela smiled back impishly. "Not really, *Hank* Fields. It's just that you taste like chicken."

Henry threw back his head and laughed. "Don't say that too loudly, or Pistol may try to take a bite out of me." At his name, Pistol opened one eye. "Let's go boy, you might as well stand up now that you're awake. Want to ride?" With amazing speed for a dog his size, Pistol leaped to his feet and was at the door instantly. "I'll take that as a yes."

After Lela called her father, Henry showed Lela the rest of the house. Much of it was left undecorated other than sparse furniture, but Lela could see the house had great potential with lots of natural light, high ceilings and golden oak floors. She shivered a little, thinking how this might one day be her home to lovingly share and fill.

They came back downstairs and Henry held the back door open to follow Lela and Pistol to the car. He opened the car door and the dog jumped in and spread himself across the back seat.

"How long have you had Pistol?" Lela asked as she climbed in the front.

"I got him when he was nine weeks old. I saw an ad in the local paper and called. The owner said they were selling the puppies cheap because they weren't purebred, and they had one male left. Back then, cheap was all I could afford, as I'd just started teaching and living on my own. I told them to consider the puppy sold and rushed right over. I should have suspected something when I asked how big they thought he'd get and they blanched. Then they explained since he wasn't pedigreed, they had no idea how big he might get. That was three years ago. Thank God he hasn't grown any in about a year."

They arrived a little early. Henry rolled the window down so Pistol could have fresh air, then he and Lela got out leaned up against the car to talk. Dread filled them as each moment passed, knowing it was almost time to part again.

Suddenly Henry stared up at the night sky. "Look!" He pointed toward a falling star that was streaking across the black velvet vastness. He turned and grabbed Lela by the shoulders. "Did you see that?"

"Yeah, it was beautiful."

"That's a sign."

"A sign of what?"

Henry sighed heavily. "I've been prayin' for a sign from God that if I needed to say this before you left me tonight He would let me know. I said, '*God, do skywritin' or something, I need to be clear on this*'. I believe that's what He just did." For a brief moment a look of frustration crossed his face. "Look, Lela, every time I leave you, it's harder. I can't think of anything else but you when we're apart. I've really been prayin' about this. A lot. I got a call yesterday, confirming that after music camp I'm going to record a Christmas CD."

"Henry, that's wonderful!"

"And one of the major networks has approached me about being part of a Christmas special they're working on, which would be a great way to promote the CD. Then there's all the holiday craziness that my family, and I assume your family, goes through."

"Yeah, so?"

"A few months after that, while I'm doing the voiceover for the movie, you'll have your first year of college out of the way, then you'll turn twenty-"

"And I won't be a teenager anymore-"

"And you won't be a teenager anymore." Henry dropped to one knee and held Lela's hand between his. "What do you say to gettin' married one year from today? Lela Sawyer, will you marry me on June twentieth, one year from today?"

She looked down into his face, his eyes bright with unshed tears. She felt tears of her own in sympathetic answer. "How could I say no? I want to be your wife. I want to be the mother of your children. Yes, Henry. Yes. I will marry you one year from today."

He jumped up, hollering like a cowboy. Pistol started barking madly, his big head bopping up and down; looking at Henry like he thought his master had lost his mind. Henry grabbed the dog's head and kissed Pistol on his muzzle. "She said yes, Pistol! She said yes!" Then he turned abruptly and kissed Lela.

"Ewwww! Henry you just kissed the *dog* and then you kissed *me!* Eww, eww! Dog slobber!"

Henry peered into her face as she wiped her mouth vigorously with the back of her hand. "Does this mean you've changed your mind?"

She grabbed his face and planted a sloppy kiss right on his mouth. "Take that, Henry Fields! And no, I've not changed my mind."

Her father pulled into the parking lot, tooting the horn at them. He stuck his head out the window, ogling the dog. "Where in the Sam Hill did you get that horse?"

Henry jogged up to the window. "That's Pistol. He just asked Lela to marry him and she said yes."

"Henry! Daddy, I did say yes. To Henry. A year from today, we're getting married."

"Well, congratulations. I'm not surprised, and I'm glad you're waiting a year. But, Lela, I don't think you should tell me until you tell your mother. Okay?"

Lela looked at her daddy and shook her head. "Men. They're *all* crazy."

Henry grabbed her again and hugged her. "I'll call you when we land. Take care of yourself. See the doctor like a good girl. I think I love you, Lela."

"Be safe, Henry. I think I love you too." She went round and got in on the passenger side of her father's car.

They waved to one another until Lela's father drove her out of sight.

Chapter Thirteen

Fifteen kids marched into class at music camp for the third day of lessons. Henry greeted them and listened to the happy chatter as they made themselves comfortable on the old rug in the center of the floor. He scooted the chair up to the edge of the circle and began to talk about the song they were learning for Friday night's assembly. He felt his cell phone vibrate in his pocket, and he absent-mindedly pulled it out and glanced down at the caller I. D. He grinned. "Guys, it's my girlfriend callin'. On the count of three yell '*Hey, Lela!*'" He pressed the on button, mouthed "One, two, three!" and the kids chorused, '*HEY, LELA!*' Henry put the phone to his ear and asked, "How did you like that?"

"Henry, it's Vicki."

His smile faded as he heard Lela's mother's voice. "Hey Vicki. What's up? Is something wrong?"

One of the little boys leaned into another kid's side and whispered, "Uh-oh. It's not Lela! It's *another* girl! I bet we got him in trouble!" They giggled.

Vicki's voice wavered. "Lela- she - she collapsed a few hours ago. We're at Piedmont Hospital. They've run some tests and are about to take her into surgery. They don't know what's wrong, but they're going to open her up."

"Open her up?" Henry repeated blankly. He felt himself weave a little on the seat. The kids in the classroom became silent as they watched Henry.

"She's in terrible pain, Henry. She was doubled over, it was so bad. They have to do exploratory surgery to find out what's wrong."

"I'll get there as soon as I can. I'll leave right now. Oh, God, Vicki, is she gonna be all right?"

"We don't know." She whispered. "We've called everyone we can think of to start praying. Henry, please hurry."

Henry hung up, staring at the kids, not really seeing them.

"Mr. Henry? Are you all right?" One of the kids asked timidly.

"I've got to go. Lela is very sick. You guys stay put and I'll send someone in. Please start prayin'!" They all solemnly nodded in obedience as he flew out the door.

He ran down the hall and grabbed the secretary as she came out of the office. He quickly explained the situation. "I've got to get on the soonest flight out -"

"Wait, Henry. My husband's a pilot. Let me see if I can catch him before he takes off. He's got a little two-seater and he can get you there in no time." She ran back into the office, returning a few moments later. "I caught him just as he was walking into the airport. He'll wait on you. He's getting clearance right now to land in Atlanta. I'll call the airport and have a rental car waiting on you."

"I hate to ask, but can you make sure they watch so I don't get stopped by somebody wantin' an autograph or something?"

She touched his arm. "Don't worry, Henry. We'll take care of everything. Just go. We'll be praying for you."

"Thanks." And he was gone.

Henry raced up the stairs of the hospital. While on the plane he had called his parents. They had promised to call Pastor James to begin a prayer chain from their church and friends. The desk clerk directed him to the appropriate hospital floor. On the elevator ride up, he tried to compose himself. He skidded to a stop at the waiting room. Lela's parents were sitting together, holding hands. Their pastor and a few friends sat with them. Vicki jumped up when she saw Henry and he grabbed her and held on tightly.

"Oh, Henry, I'm so glad you're here." She pulled away and mopped at her eyes.

"It seems like it took forever. Where is Lela now?"

Lela's father spoke up. "She's in surgery. We don't know anything yet." He glanced down at the floor. "She said to tell you she loves you."

Henry turned his back for a moment, head down, eyes closed. How could things go so horribly wrong so quickly? *Please God, I know we're supposed to pray for Your will, but please save her! Don't take her home, let me have her here for now, please!"*

Henry looked up as his parents and Pastor James walked into the waiting room.

Henry was about to explain to them what he knew, when a doctor came in. "Mr. and Mrs. Sawyer?"

The room became totally still as all eyes turned on him. He glanced at the small group of people. Lela's father said, "Please, just tell us. These are all friends and family. They need to hear too."

The doctor nodded. He sat down and leaned forward, his arms resting on his knees. "She's in recovery. The news isn't good. I've never seen such a severe case of endometriosis. It had invaded her ovaries, her uterus and part of her intestine. She had also developed an ovarian cyst from it. All the pain she's been complaining about probably had nothing to do with her accident or surgery, but was symptomatic of the endometriosis and complications from it. The acute pain came when the cyst ruptured. Also, a small tear occurred while removing scar tissue from the intestine, but we repaired that and the intestine seems healthy. I don't think there'll be any complications from it." He seemed to choose his next words carefully, glancing at Henry. "She'll never be able to have children. We had to do a total hysterectomy. We did manage to save a tiny piece of one ovary, hoping she won't need hormone replacement therapy if she recovers."

Lela's mother gasped. "What do you mean *if* she recovers?" She grabbed her husband's arm.

"She had some heart arrhythmia during surgery. We thought we had it stabilized, but it happened again. She's not responding. I don't know if the arrhythmias have caused the lack of response. I don't see why it would." He looked at them. "I'm sorry I can't tell you why this has happened. I'm sorry I can't tell you if she'll wake up, and if she does at what level she will function." He stood. "I'm going back to check on her now. I'll let you know when you can see her." He nodded to everyone, and then walked out.

No one moved. No one spoke.

Chapter Fourteen

Two days went by. Lela was breathing on her own, but did not regain consciousness. Her parents took turns sitting by her bed, Henry often with them. They alternated going to Henry's house to shower and eat an occasional meal other than hospital food. Friends kept constant vigil and people were assigned prayer time around the clock. The doctors reported no sign of change, nor could they find any reason for Lela's unresponsiveness.

Henry walked down the hospital corridor and stood at the end where a bank of windows looked out over a small grassy area with potted flowers on each side of a park bench. A young couple sat, basking in the sun. They were holding hands. Even though Henry could only see the back of their heads, he could tell they were deep into conversation and body language indicated they were attuned to one another very well. He leaned his head against the glass, feeling tears prick his eyelids. His fists clenched until he could feel the sting of his nails biting into his palms. All he could see was Lela's face, placid as a deep lake, unmoving and unmoved. Except for the rise and fall of the sheet that covered her body, one wouldn't know if she was still living. He desperately tried to pray, but no words came. He tried to believe that the Holy Spirit would understand the groaning of his soul and interpret his desire to the Heavenly Father, for Henry knew of no words that could ever convey his sorrow and grief.

His cell phone rang and he dug it out of his pocket to answer.

"Henry? How are you?" It was Pastor James.

"Alone. Afraid. Angry. Lela's still the same."

"I want to suggest something to you. I don't know Lela's parents well, but they seem to be Christ centered people. I do know without a doubt they want their daughter healed. I've talked with their pastor, and we are in agreement that he and the elders need to anoint Lela and lay hands on her for healing. He's calling Lela's father now." Pastor James paused for a moment, waiting for a reply, but Henry remained silent. "I know Lela isn't your wife, but because of your intentions, we felt we should invite you to be present also. If her parents approve and request the service, will you be a part too?"

"I want that. But I'm so angry with God. Why did He allow this to happen? Why would He bring us together and then take her away?"

"All things happen to His children for His glory, Henry. The Book of James, in Chapter 5 says: '*Is any one of you sick? He should call the elders of the church to pray over him and anoint him with oil in the name of the Lord. And the prayer offered in faith will make the sick person well, the Lord will raise him up. If he has sinned, he will be forgiven. Therefore; confess your sin to one another and pray for one another so you may be healed. The prayer of a righteous man is powerful and effective.*' Well, Lela can't call us right now and request this. But her mama and daddy can. Her future husband can. Will you step out on faith and join us, Henry?"

Henry turned as he heard footsteps behind him. It was Lela's mother. She had the phone in her hand, tears running down her face. She looked at him with hope in her eyes. He hadn't seen hope there since the doctor's words days ago. He smiled at her. "Yes, I will step out on faith, James. As much as we love Lela, I know that God loves her more. I'll be there."

"Good boy. Never give up, son. God loves you too. He's there for you and will give you comfort if you let Him. Don't let anger get in the way of it. I'll talk to you soon."

"All right. And thanks. Thanks so much." Henry hung up and turned to Vicki. "I gather you've talked to your preacher too."

"He's going to call us back as soon as they can get a time set for all the elders to be here. I wanted to make sure you knew, too." She was pressing numbers on her phone. "I'm going to start calling friends and ask them to be on stand by so they can stop and pray wherever they are when the time comes." She grasped Henry's hand. "There is power in prayer, Henry. Let's begin to pray for our faith to be increased and for God to show us any unconfessed sin so we'll be ready when the time comes." She squeezed his hand before letting go and turning back down the hall.

"Vicki?" She turned back toward him and waited. "I'm goin' home for a little while." Henry dropped his eyes. "I'm not ready. I'm so angry! I feel selfish because I haven't thought about what's best for Lela or even you and Art. I just want what I want, and I want Lela. Can you forgive me?"

"Oh, Henry, there's nothing to forgive. Don't you think I've struggled with the very same thing? I haven't cared one whit what anybody else wanted, *especially* God. I was afraid He might want Lela with Him." She shrugged. "And maybe He does. But I'm not giving her up unless He tells me to. I think we need to follow the direction He's given us in scripture to find out what He desires. We all have to prepare for that. Not just you." She reached out and patted his arm. "Go on home. Rest a little and pray a lot. Get prepared for this. We'll see you back soon."

Henry nodded and watched her turn again toward the waiting area. He ran his hand through his hair, fished out his car keys and headed for home.

He pulled into his driveway forty-five minutes later, and sat in the car, motionless. He couldn't seem to find the energy to move. He stared at his house, something he had been proud of and thankful for. He felt nothing now. Singing hadn't entered his mind in days. His agent had called at some point, but he barely remembered what was said. Ted had kept in touch and some of the musicians he'd toured with called. He felt nothing for any of it. Slowly he climbed out of the car and made his way into the house. The phone light was blinking. He glanced down. He had twenty-seven messages waiting. He walked into the kitchen and opened the refrigerator. He grabbed a Coke and took a few swigs of it, absent-mindedly noticing the plethora of food prepared and neatly wrapped, waiting on someone who actually had an appetite.

As he walked through his house it seemed as though it echoed with every step. He felt like a stranger in his own home, as hollow and empty as if it had been stripped of furniture and he of life.

Henry fell across the bed, dry eyed and spent. The house was as quiet as a tomb; the only thing he could hear was the faint ticking of the grandfather's clock in the foyer. Finally, he spoke out loud. "I don't know what to say, Lord. I feel like a little kid who is furious with his daddy 'cause he didn't get his way. I want to have a tantrum. Would too, if I didn't feel so exhausted. I don't think I can talk to You cause I'm so mad at You."

'My grace is sufficient.'

"I know. But right now I don't feel Your grace."

"*Fear not. Be anxious for nothing. I am with you always, even unto the ends of the earth.*"

"Are You sayin' I'm more scared than mad?" Henry thought on that for a moment and slowly nodded his head. "You're right. I am absolutely freaking scared out of my mind." His chin trembled. "I've never loved anybody like this. If I lose her I don't know what I'll do. You're supposed to be all I need, and I thought I believed that. I didn't mean to put her before You. Is that what I've done? If it is, I'm sorry. I don't know how to change that, I don't know how not to be afraid. I need a little help here, Lord. I'm a royal mess." And with that, Henry closed his eyes and fell into a deep to sleep.

The dream began with him walking in a dark forest. The sun occasionally blinked in and out of the heavy canopy, but Henry was mostly in shadows. He could hear someone crying, and he was frantically looking for them. He was sure if he could just find them, he could help. The wind picked up and he thought he heard thunder in the distance. His urgency increasing, he began to run. As he topped a ridge, the crying became louder, and he looked down into a hollow. Henry stared in disbelief. He was looking at himself! He was on his knees, sobbing and wailing as though the end of time was near. 'Henry! Henry Fields!' he yelled to himself. His other self looked up, face tear streak, nose running. 'Who are you? What do you want?' Henry was shocked. 'It's me! Don't you recognize me? It's Hank. What's the matter, why are you crying?' Henry stood up and wiped his face on his sleeve. 'Don't you know? Haven't you heard? It's over, Hank. Pack up and move on. You ain't singin' no more.' He stood there, trying to figure out how this had happened without him knowing. Had they cancelled the concerts when he wasn't paying attention? As he opened his mouth to ask, he heard someone else begin to cry. He whirled around and saw Lela. She was in the middle of the forest, lying in an old-fashioned iron hospital bed. The bed shook with the force of her sobbing. He started skidding down the hill, slipping on leaves, trying not to fall, when he crashed up against the bed. Lela's eyes flew open and she stared at him. 'Where's Henry? I don't want you! I want Henry!' He ran his hands through his hair. Wasn't he Henry and Hank both? How could she love one and not the other? 'I'm Henry too, Lela, remember?' She raised up on one elbow and looked into his eyes, unblinking. Then she broke into her beautiful smile that he hadn't seen in so long. 'Henry! It's you! My sweet uber goober!' Laughing, he asked, 'What did you call me?' Suddenly a ringing filled the air and they both turned to find the source. It rang again, and again…

Henry sat up with a jerk. His heart was pounding and the bedside phone was ringing.

"Henry? Did I wake you up? You sound right funny."

He fell back on the bed. "Hey Papa. Yeah. One minute I was prayin' and the next minute I was havin' the weirdest dream I ever had."

Asa grunted. "Sometimes dreams mean a lot and sometimes they're just foolishness. Did it mean somethin' to you?"

Henry thought a moment. "You tell me." He explained what he remembered.

Asa cackled. "What does 'uber' mean?"

"Very. You know, like you're uber handsome."

"Ah, boy, I can still whip your tail if I need to. Sounds to me like you just needed affirmation that Lela loves all the pieces of you. But I'm glad I caught you at home, 'cause I can't find that cell phone number you give me. Your mama called and said they's havin' a healin' service for Lela. 'Bout time, I say. You call me soon as you find out when. My little church fambly will want to be in on the prayin'. I believe there's power in numbers, and the more we got prayin' when the anointin's being done, the better." Asa's voice lost some of its' feistiness. "How you doin', boy? I been prayin' night and day for you too. It's hard on you, ain't it?"

"Papa, I'm so afraid."

"Now, looky here, son. It's all right. When your Gramms died, I wanted to die too. Fact is, I laid down and told the Lord to take me right then. I got so dadgummed mad at Him for not listenin' to me! I figured what use was an old codger like me, with nobody to share this house and probably soon to be a burden on my own child? Well, thankfully, the good Lord don't make it a habit of listenin' to fools, and I'm still here. He's blessed me beyond measure these few years since. And your Gramms woulda knocked me sideways if I'd showed up ahead of time, missin' the ride of success you've had." Asa's voice softened. "Don't be too hard on yourself, son. The Lord understands. But He also knows what we don't. Your Lela is in His hand, just like we all are. Don't be goin' and try to take her out."

Henry had forgotten how much he loved his Papa. "You always know exactly what I need to hear, Papa. How could I forget He's got Lela right where she needs to be, and that makes it fine? You better hang around a few more years, cause obviously I ain't got enough sense to make it without you yet."

"I plan on hangin' around some. You don't forget to call me now."

"I won't. As soon as I know the time, I'll call you first. I love you Papa."

"I love you too, boy."

Henry stretched and sat up. He glanced at the clock and was surprised that he'd been asleep an hour. He thought about the dream, and guessed Asa was right. Then he grinned. *Uber goober!* Where had his subconscious come up with that? Wait till Lela heard that phrase. His smile faded a little. "Lord, please let her hear it soon." He trudged back to the kitchen and got cold cuts out for a sandwich. Food and a shower should make him feel better and then he could get back to the hospital.

The phone rang again. This time it was Vicki. "Henry, the pastor and elders will be here at the hospital tomorrow morning at eleven." She choked up a little. "All six elders are taking off work. They said this didn't need to wait till evening."

"I'll call my folks and they can let everyone know to be in prayer at that time. What did the hospital say when you told them?"

"The charge nurse didn't like it. She said it would be a disturbance on the hall, but Lela's doctor overrode her. He said the Great Physician was on staff here too."

"Good for the doc. I'm about to eat and take a quick shower then come on back. There's plenty of food here, so tell Art not to eat that hospital junk. I'll be back in a couple of hours."

Henry hung up and called Asa as well as the rest as he wolfed down his sandwich. On the way to the shower, he stopped by his bed and dropped to his knees. "Thanks for changin' me. Thanks for people who love Lela and love You enough to believe. I'm like the fellow in the Bible, Lord: I believe, help me with my unbelief! I don't have much faith, but what I have is in You."

"It is enough."

Henry nodded his head in agreement, then headed for the shower.

Chapter Fifteen

*H*enry arrived back at the hospital around ten thirty that morning, having gone home again in the middle of the night to sleep. Art and Vicki had slept some at his house earlier in the evening and had insisted he get a solid block of sleep too. He was nervous, almost like before going on stage. He rose at eight to read the Bible and pray, asking God to show him any unconfessed sin. He supposed he was as ready as he was ever going to be, and a certain calm had engulfed him.

Entering the lobby, he was surprised to find Vicki and Art waiting. His heart gave a lurch – had something happened to Lela before the elders could get there to pray? But when they saw him and smiled, he relaxed.

Lela's father said, "We thought we'd meet you down here. I guess everyone is so excited they got here early. It's getting a little crowded up there. We wanted to have prayer with you before we go up."

Henry looked from Art to Vicki. "I love you guys so much. Thank you for letting me be a part of this."

They joined hands as Art prayed aloud, asking God to bless the service and to fill their hearts with His love and acceptance of His will. He thanked God for Lela and for allowing them to have her in their lives.

They rode up on the elevator. Walking into the waiting area, Henry was shocked to see so many people. Tears filled his eyes as he saw his parents and Asa, Ted and Susan and many other friends and fellow church members. Emmie was smiling at him through tears. Other people milled around Henry did not know. Pastor James was standing by Lela's pastor.

When they saw Henry and Lela's parents, they rose in one accord, standing shoulder to shoulder. Lela's pastor stepped forward. He placed himself between Vicki and Art and spoke quietly to the crowd. "We are here to represent Lela Sawyer. She is unable to request anointing and the laying on of hands, but we are her brothers and sisters in Christ, and we request it for her."

"Amen." The crowd rumbled.

"There are many people who aren't in this room who are preparing themselves right now for prayer." He turned to Henry. "Your high school gymnasium is completely full as we speak. All three of the church houses represented here are full. Lela's high school auditorium is full too. There are people who couldn't get to any of those places who will stop what they're doing beginning at eleven to pray. Most of the businesses back home will cease operation for ten minutes at eleven o'clock sharp so their employees can pray. I am humbled to know all this. I am truly blessed to be a witness to such an event. Brother James, if you will step forward to lead the prayer with all these good people in here, the family and elders will proceed to Lela's room."

As Henry left the waiting room, he looked over at his family. His father was holding onto to his mother's hand. Asa smiled tearfully at Henry and gave him a thumbs up.

He heard, rather than saw, all those left begin to get on their knees.

Entering Lela's room, Henry could not hold back his tears. The room filled with natural light, making red sparks dance in Lela's hair. Her hands lay at her sides. Her face was undisturbed and her breathing even. The nurse looked up as they opened the door. Her mouth was set in a thin line of disapproval. She glanced at Lela, then quickly left the room.

The elders gathered around the hospital bed. The pastor stood at Lela's head. Henry took one of Lela's hands; Vicki and Art took the other. The elders all placed their hands on Lela's arms or lower legs. The pastor opened a small vial of oil to be used for anointing. He bowed his head. "Father, we ask You in the name of Your Son, Jesus Christ, to bless this." He gently rubbed oil on Lela's forehead. Laying the vial aside, he placed his hands on her head. "Father, Your children have come today to stand boldly before Your throne to represent Lela. Lord, she has led a faithful life. She lovingly serves You. She has been faithful to her parent's belief and has taken on that belief herself. She has believed that You placed Henry in her life in order for them to have a future as man and wife. Your Word says that if one of us is sick, we are to gather the elders together and follow the direction scripture gives us so the sick may be healed. We have done so. All of us here, Father, have earnestly searched our hearts. We have confessed any sin and repented. We trust in the almighty blood of Jesus Christ for forgiveness. And now, Father, we ask in the name of Your Son, Jesus Christ, to heal Lela Sawyer from this unnatural sleep. Heal her now, Lord!"

The room hummed with amens as the pastor ended the prayer. They all looked up. Henry studied Lela's still face as he bent to kiss her. He felt the oil on his lips as he brushed her forehead. Raising up, he was suddenly staring into her eyes.

"Hey Henry." Lela's voice was rusty from lack of use. When she heard her mother gasp, she turned her head. "Mama?" She looked around the room. "What's everyone doing in here? Is my operation over?"

Pandemonium, to say the least, ensued.

Chapter Sixteen

After a second of stunned silence, grown men began to whoop and holler, Lela's mother was praising the name of Jesus and Lela was looking at them with incredulity.

The door swiftly pushed open as the charge nurse came in, a look of fury on her face. "What's the meaning of this noise? Don't you know you're disturbing the whole floor? Oh!" She stopped dead in her tracks, hand to her heart as she saw Lela's open eyes. She whirled around and ran back out of the room.

One of the elders darted out right behind her, and Henry could hear him yelling, "She's healed! She's awake! God woke her up!" A cheer went up in the waiting room.

The door banged open and Lela's doctor strode in. He grinned from ear to ear and bent over Lela. "Hello, young lady! About time you re-joined us. I hear our Heavenly Father's been busy." He gently turned her head and peered into her eyes, touched her face with reverence, listened to her heart and laughed out loud. "I have no idea what I'm doing!" He shook his head. "Praise God." He said softly. He turned to Lela's parents. "Let's leave these two love birds alone for a moment, shall we?" He smiled and escorted them out of the room.

"Henry, what in the world happened?"

He smiled down at her. "Oh, just a little miracle, my love." His eyes filled with tears. "Your surgery was four days ago, Lela. No matter what the doctors tried, you didn't wake up. Everyone you and I know and plenty we don't have been praying night and day for you. Our pastors got a service together. Pastor James stayed in the waiting room with a hundred or so of your closest friends and prayed with them while your elders and pastor came in here and anointed you with oil, laid hands on you and asked God to heal you."

"Wow." Lela searched Henry's face. "Was my surgery successful? Was all the pain related to my injury?"

Henry blinked. He was in no way prepared to answer this. He hadn't even *thought* of her surgery in days. "It wasn't related to your injury."

When he hesitated before saying more, she grasped his arm and looked intently at his face. "Is it cancer?"

"What?" Henry asked in surprise. "Oh, honey, no! You don't have cancer. I didn't mean to scare you. It's just that we have been so afraid you were never gonna wake up that your surgery sort of took a back seat in my thinkin'." He took a deep breath. He knew it wasn't his place to say much. "I think the doctor is just a little more qualified to talk about your surgery than me, but I believe it was a success."

Lela looked relieved. "I don't know why, but I was getting so worried just before they brought me here. I was beginning to think I had ovarian cancer or something."Before she could finish her thought, her parents stepped back into the room.

They were all smiles as they patted and kissed their child. After a few more reassuring touches, Lela's mother spoke up. "Honey, the three of us are going to have to take a hike. The doctor insists on a full examination." She smiled down at Lela. "The nurse is coming in to give you medications and change your bandage."

A beaming nurse came in carrying a tray of supplies. She waited while Henry and Lela's parents said a quick good-bye. As they exited the room, they heard the nurse talking cheerfully to Lela.

They walked down the hall to the now empty waiting room. "We need to talk, son." Art said. "The doctor wants Lela to have a few days to recuperate before they explain to her about the hysterectomy. He says she's in no shape to hear that right now. They're going to put her on mild sedatives for a few days, so maybe she'll be too sleepy to ask a lot of questions. She needs to rest a lot in order to heal quickly."

"She asked me if the surgery was successful and if she had cancer. I reassured her she was cancer free and that the operation was successful. Do you think that was all right?"

Vicki nodded agreement. "I think that was perfect. My poor little chick! I'm so glad you told her it wasn't cancer."

They stood up to go. "I think Vicki and I are going to stick around for a little while, then we may actually sleep in our own bed tonight." He put his arm around his wife's shoulders. "Frankly, if we talk to Lela much, she'll get suspicious when there are no details forthcoming from us. That goes for you too, Henry."

"Who else knows what the surgery entailed?" Henry asked.

"Our pastors, the few friends that were here when the doctor came to talk to us after surgery and you, unless you told others."

"I haven't even told my parents. I was so scared about her not waking up, the other stuff has never really registered enough to tell." He ran his hand through his hair. "I want you to know it doesn't matter to me either. I love Lela, no matter what." He closed his eyes. "When I think we might have lost her, I can hardly bear it. I'm by her side, always."

They did an awkward group hug, sniffing back tears. They joined hands, said a quick prayer and Henry told them good-bye.

Walking to his car, he heard a female voice call, "Hank! Hank Fields!"

He closed his eyes in dread. *'Not now, Lord, I'm too tired to sign autographs.'* he thought, but turned toward the voice, plastering a smile on his face. To his surprise it was the frowning, disapproving charge nurse who had fought the healing service at every turn. She rushed up to him and laid her hand on his arm.

"You must tell me, Hank!"

He looked at her, confused. "Tell you what?"

"Who is this Jesus?" She asked urgently. "I have to know, please tell me."

Henry looked into her eyes and gave her a genuine smile this time. "If you've got a few minutes, I will be more than happy to tell you about Him. I know a lot, 'cause He's my best friend."

She nodded ascent as they headed back to the hospital and into the cafeteria.

When he left, Henry knew he'd never think of her as the frowning, disapproving nurse again.

Chapter Seventeen

As the next few days passed, Henry was impressed at how well oiled the hospital staff had become at interrupting conversation in Lela's room. He didn't know how her parents felt, but it gave him a great sense of relief. He could tell she was becoming suspicious because so little information was given regarding her surgery.

Lela was telling him about Emmie coming by. "She asked me about the surgery and I felt so foolish when I couldn't tell her anything. I don't think I realized how little I knew until that moment." Lela was raised to a sitting position in the bed. She carefully crossed her arms over her chest. "Henry Fields, I am not stupid. I want to know *right now* what's going on!"

Henry opened his mouth, with no idea of what he was going to say, when the door popped open and the doctor walked in.

Lela glared at him. "Why is it when I try to have a conversation with anybody I am rudely interrupted every single time?"

"I can see you're feeling better." The doctor said cheerfully.

As Lela's eyes began to narrow, Henry stood up quickly. He glanced at the doctor and nodded his head toward Lela. "That's my cue to leave. When she squints her eyes, you better watch out."

"Coward." The doctor grinned.

"You better believe it."

"Look, I just want to know what's going on. Are you going to tell me or do I demand to see my chart?"

"Take it easy, Lela. You can blame me for all the evasive tactics, if there were any. I instructed your family to keep their mouths shut until you'd had a few days to recover." He walked over to the bed and placed his hands on the rails. "You were in a lot of danger there for a few days and I wanted you stronger before I went all technical on you."

She gave a curt nod. "Now I'm better. So talk."

He raised his eyebrows and looked at Henry. "I see what you mean about watching out. But I think I can handle it from here." He turned back to Lela. "Believe it or not, I actually was coming in here to do exactly that. Talk, I mean."

Henry bent and kissed Lela's forehead. "I'll see you later."

Lela smiled at him. "Don't go too far."

"I won't." His gaze was intense. "I never will."

Her parents were in the waiting room. They looked apprehensive as Henry sat down next to them. "Did the doctor call you?"

"Yes," Art said. "He felt like we needed to be close by. Who knows how she's going to take this?"

A half hour passed. Running out of small talk, they were just sitting, fidgeting, waiting on the doctor. Relief mingled with fear filled all three as they searched the doctor's face when he finally joined them. He sat down, wearily rubbing a hand over his eyes. "She didn't take it well. She's very, very upset. I threatened to give her a sedative if she didn't calm down. That seemed to help, and she started asking questions. She wants to see you now."

The three stood, but the doctor stopped Henry. "Just her parents. She specifically said she couldn't face you yet."

Art patted Henry on the back. "We'll be back. Sit tight. Talk to him, doc."

As they walked out, Henry turned to the doctor. "What am I supposed to say to her? As long as she's well, I can deal with anything else. I want her to know I love her regardless."

"Sounds like a good place to start." He stood, arching his back, stretching. "There's no way to gage how a woman will react when she finds she is suddenly unable to have babies. I assume you two had discussed having a family?"

"Many times." Henry started pacing. "I hope that doesn't make her think it's more important than it really is."

"Henry, it *is* important. Don't kid yourself into believing this won't make a difference. It's not just an adjustment for Lela. Right now you are so thankful that she's alive you haven't had room to feel anything else. But you can't shove your feelings aside and pretend it doesn't matter whether you get to be a father or not. If you've always assumed, like Lela has, that your future includes children, you're going to have to deal with your own feelings."

"I guess you're right, but I feel so protective of her. I can't let Lela see me hurting about this."

"I think that's exactly what you should do."

Henry shook his head. "Maybe later. But now, I'm going to be strong for her."

They turned as Lela's parents re-entered. Vicki had been crying. Art was pale as he looked at Henry. "You need to go on home, Henry. She's flatly refusing to see you tonight."

"I need to see her, I need to tell her it's going to be all right - "

"Henry, she's too upset. She's not listening to reason. She wouldn't listen to us." Vicki started crying again. "She's saying all sorts of foolish things, she says her life is over, she'll never marry - "

"*What?*" Henry started in surprise. "She can't mean that. We've got our whole lives ahead of us, it's not over!"

The doctor spoke up. "Look, I'll order a sedative for her tonight. She's got to calm down, and she needs to sleep. I'll send the hospital chaplain in to speak to her. Maybe things will look brighter for her in the morning."

Henry walked Vicki and Art to their car, all of them silent. Vicki hugged him quickly before getting in and Art patted him on the back.

Henry felt like he was on an emotional roller coaster that was never going to stop.

Henry went home, called his agent and told him to cancel any appointments for the next two weeks, and he'd get back to him after that. His agent assured him that his schedule was pretty clear for now, but stressed he had to get with the record company regarding the upcoming Christmas CD soon. Henry barely heard him, and found little inside of himself that cared.

He called his parents and told them the entire truth about Lela's surgery and asked them to pray harder than ever. His mother cried as she recalled the emergency hysterectomy she'd had after Henry was born. "But at least I had you. I don't know what I would have done if there hadn't been you."

He called Pastor James and let him know Lela was having a difficult time and asked for the pastor to start the prayer chain. Pastor James assured him he'd do that and folks would be praying not only for Lela, but for him too.

Henry took a hot shower and went to bed. He lay awake for hours, alternately punching the pillow and turning from his stomach to his back.

He awoke with a start and blearily looked at the clock. It was almost six. He had been dreaming that Lela was telling him she'd changed her mind, and was going to marry Hank instead. "What is wrong with me?" He muttered. "I can't get this whole Henry/Hank thing out of my mind and I never even thought about it till Lela complained."

He shuffled to the bathroom, but sprinted back when the phone rang. "Please let it be Lela, please let it be Lela!" he prayed as he dove for the cordless.

He grabbed the phone and yelled, "Hello!" into it.

"I hope I didn't wake you up, but I needed to talk and you were the only person I could think of."

"Who is this?" Henry asked, perplexed.

"Sorry. It's Emmie." She started crying. "Lela would hardly talk to me and she said she wasn't talking to you either."

"You called her at this hour?" *'No wonder she wouldn't talk'* He thought.

"No, no. I called her yesterday, just after you left the hospital. She was upset and angry and accused me of keeping the results of her surgery a secret from her! I told her I *still* didn't know why she had surgery; we'd all been so upset about her not waking up I'd forgot to ask! She didn't believe me. When I promised her I had no idea, she told me. Henry, is it true? She can't have babies?"

He sat down on the edge of the bed. "Yeah. It's true."

"How awful! She's always talked about being a mama. We played dolls for hours when we were little girls." Emmie hesitated. "Are – are you okay?"

"Well, I thought I was till she refused to see me after the doctor gave her the news. I haven't been okay since." He plowed his hand through his hair. "I thought I had lost her, and then in the middle of rejoicin' that I hadn't, she refuses to see me. Man, I'm so messed up I don't know if I'm comin' or goin'."

"I know she really loves you, Henry. Try not to worry too much. She'll come round. I mean, she hung up on me and said she'd call me when she was ready to talk. It's not like she's singling you out."

"Maybe you're right. I can't stand this for long though." His phone chimed. "Emmie, I've got another call comin' in. I'll talk to you later." He clicked the phone. "Hello?"

"Hey."

He sagged with relief. "Oh, Lela, it's so good to hear your voice. You scared me so badly when you wouldn't see me yesterday."

"Sorry. Um, Henry, would you mind not coming to the hospital for a few days?"

His heart picked up speed. "Why? Lela, we've got to work this out. I want us to talk."

"I know you want to talk. I'm sorry for making you wait." Her voice caught. "I j-just can't right now. Please don't make me." He heard her sob.

"Shhh, now, Lela, it's all right. I won't make you do anything you don't want to do. I didn't mean to sound impatient. I just miss you so much. I want you to know I'm here for you." He said quietly, "I want to hold on to you and never let you go."

She was silent for a few seconds. He heard her blow her nose. "Henry, I promise I'll talk to you as soon as I can. But right now, I need to think about all this. I don't even want to see Daddy, but I'm afraid I'll hurt his feelings. I j-just want Mama."

He felt his heart breaking for her. "I understand. Your daddy will too. Just tell him. He loves you, and so do I."

"You don't think he'll be hurt?"

"Nah. He'd do anything for you, you know that. I promise he'll wait until you're ready to see him and won't get a bit hurt."

"Will you tell him for me?"

Henry felt himself smile. "I'll tell him for you. Man to man. We'll both wait on you. We'll wait for as long as you need us to."

"Okay."

"Anything else you want me to do for you?"

"I guess not. They're coming in with my breakfast tray now, so I'll go."

"Call me soon, Lela."

"I will. Thanks Henry."

"You're welcome. I think I love you, Lela."

But she'd already hung up.

Chapter Eighteen

Three days passed. Henry kept in touch with Lela's parents, but they knew little. They had encouraged Lela to talk with their pastor or Bible Study teacher. She had agreed, but it seemed little had changed.

When her mother tried to reason with her, Lela became angry and said she'd see Henry when she was ready.

Only a day had gone by before she was asking for her father, and the next day she had seen Emmie too. Lela had spoken briefly with her pastor, but didn't share what they had discussed. She was being secretive with everyone.

When Lela finally called Henry, she was brief and distant. She simply told him she was going to be discharged in a day, and requested he visit her before then. He tried to tease and ask her if it would be like "old times" when he had first visited her at the hospital in New York. She had not shared in the banter and had quickly ended the conversation.

Now he stood in the hospital parking lot, afraid of going in. He gave himself a good mental shake and strode through the grounds and into the hospital. His finger shook as he pressed the elevator button.

Passing by the nurse's station, he heard a familiar voice say, "We've missed you around here." He turned, and saw the now smiling charge nurse.

"Thanks." He nodded toward Lela's door. "How is she?"

"It's hard to say. She's not talked much. I think she's very sad. But maybe getting to go home this afternoon will cheer her up. And I'm sure your visit will too."

"Let's hope so. How are you?"

"I'm great. Thank you for talking with me. I started church last Sunday! It's like a whole new world has opened up to me."

"You'll never be the same."

Another nurse muttered, "Thank God for that," and everyone burst into laughter.

Henry walked on down the hall, threw back his shoulders, and saying a quick prayer, knocked on Lela's door.

She was sitting in a chair. Her hands were folded neatly in her lap and her hair was pulled back from her face. She glanced at him nervously when he entered the room, then quickly dropped her eyes.

He stopped, standing in front of her, his heart thumping wildly in his chest. He was absolutely terrified because she looked anything but welcoming.

"Sit down, Henry, you're making me nervous."

He sat in the other chair, turning it to face her directly. "It's so good to see you sittin' up instead of in the bed. I guess you're feelin' a lot better."

She shrugged. "They've had me walking the halls and they've lectured me into staying up so I can be discharged."

There was uneasy silence for a few moments until Henry cleared his throat. "Am I the lucky one to take you home?"

She looked surprised at that. "No, Daddy's coming at two o'clock. The nurse said the doctor should be through with rounds by then." She glanced at him. "Have you spoken with them lately?"

"You mean your parents?" She nodded. "I've just about driven them crazy. Haven't they told you how much I've called?"

"Yes. I meant, have they told you what I've said?"

Henry shifted in his chair. "I don't know that they've shared everything, but they've been distressed over some of the things you've told them." He chewed his lower lip. "I know this has been a shock for you, it's no wonder they've worried about your reaction to all this."

She set her mouth in a thin line. "They don't believe a word I've said. But I've meant *every* word. That's why I wanted to talk to you here, before I go home." She finally looked him in the eye. "I don't want to see you anymore, Henry. I'm not going to marry you and it's not fair to have you believe that for a minute longer."

"You can't mean that Lela, you're just upset over what has happened."

"It's worse than upset, Henry. My world has changed forever. I'm nineteen years old and part of my life is over. I'll never be the same."

Henry slid from the chair and crouched in front of her, balancing himself with his hand on her chair. "You're right, you'll never be the same. But you're still you. And it's you I love. I can't imagine my life without you, Lela. Outside of salvation, you're the best gift God has ever given me."

"Well, get used to life without me, Henry. You've lived most of your life without knowing I even existed. It won't be that hard to go back."

He shook his head. "Will it be that easy for you to move forward without me? Just because a few months ago you didn't know I existed?"

"I don't expect anything to be easy again. I don't care if I *never* move forward. Before, I always thought life was about moving forward. You know, you grow up, fall in love, get married and have kids. Progression. Well, I guess the joke is on me, huh?"

"Just because we can't have kids doesn't mean we can't still be a family."

"Not *we* Henry, *me*. You can have kids, I can't."

"Two can be a very good family. You're all the family I need."

"I don't believe that. We've talked many times about having children. I've seen the desire in your eyes. I know how you feel about kids. You were going to *teach* for heaven's sake."

"I'll adjust. *We'll* adjust. We'll get counseling and postpone the wedding until you're better."

"I'm done with counseling, Henry. I want you to leave me alone. I'm not going to see you any more."

"Can you look me in the eye and say you don't love me?"

Her lip trembled. "You know I love you. My decision has nothing to do with not loving you. You deserve better than I can give you."

"I don't want it any other way, Lela. I want you."

"Go away Henry."

"No! I'm not gonna just walk out of here like I'm in some lame movie scene. This is real life, Lela. I won't abandon you."

"You're right about one thing. This isn't a movie. Movies have happy endings. But you're wrong if you think I'm going to change my mind."

"Have you even prayed about this?"

"I seem to be done praying, too. At least I can't hear Him." She bowed her head. "Maybe I'm too mad or hurt right now to hear. Maybe someday I'll hear God's voice again." She shrugged. "Right now it doesn't even matter to me."

"Well, it matters to me. And it matters to God. Can we pray together right now?"

"No!" Lela looked panicked. "Stop trying to get your way. Just *go* away."

"Stop being pigheaded, Lela."

"If I have to call security, I will Henry." Her voice became very quiet. "I mean it. Don't call me any more, don't try to see me any more."

He ran his hand through his hair as he stood up in frustration. "You're being so childish! I mean, why would we even *need* to have kids if *you're* gonna act like one all the time!"

His eyes widened and Lela's narrowed as he realized what he'd said aloud. He tensed, ready for the tirade to begin, but instead, Lela's shoulders slumped. He instantly reached for her, but she held her hands up to ward him off. "Please, please don't touch me, Henry." Tears began to course down her cheeks. "I don't believe I could take it."

"Lela -"

"If you love me like you say you do, you'll go. Please Henry, just leave."

He nodded once, turned, and walked out.

Behind the door that Henry closed, Lela doubled over, racked with sobs. The hardest day of her life had been when they told her she would never have children.

Until today.

Chapter Nineteen

enry drove mindlessly, occasionally remembering to slow down when he glanced at the speedometer.

He had sat in the parking lot for a while, staring at his cell phone, desperate to talk to someone, anyone.

But who?

His parents would be as upset as he, and he needed comforting.

Lela's parents? What could they say to him? He knew they had tried to convince Lela to wait before making any kind of decisions.

All of his friends had rejoiced with him when he'd found Lela, prayed with him when she'd taken ill, praised God with Him when she'd awakened from surgery and grieved with him when they found out about her condition. How could he possibly ask them to listen to him one more time?

He didn't feel close enough to Emmie to start up a conversation this intense and he didn't think he could take another shattered female right now, anyway.

So he'd put his phone away, unused. Prayer did not come either. Not even a '*Why, God?*' Just mindlessness.

When he stopped driving he wasn't really surprised to find himself parked in front of his grandfather's house. It was late in the afternoon, the sun was already going behind the house a bit, leaving it dappled in tree leafed shadows. He sat there staring at the house, hearing the engine tick as it cooled down. Asa's house was a miniature of the house Henry had built for himself.

As a child, Henry had spent countless days in the yard and countless nights in the tiny attic bedroom, sleeping in an old iron bed tucked underneath the window, opened in the summer to let in nighttime breezes. Summer nights were the nights he recalled the most vividly. Insects and tree frogs made so much noise; he'd put a pillow over his head to try and sleep, eventually giving up because the pillow made him hotter than ever. He'd plant his hands under his head and lean sideways, peering out the window at the night sky, wondering just how far up among the stars God lived. He recalled one late fall night he'd fallen asleep like that, only to awaken hours later, freezing. He had looked at his bed in disbelief. The sheet was covered in a fine dusting of snow. In his excitement, he'd leaped from the bed hollering for Papa and Gramms as he ran down the stairs, scaring them badly.

When he had built his bigger, finer house, this one had stayed in his mind's eye as he attempted to capture the home he felt here.

'And for what?' He thought now.

Henry always had faith that God had his mate picked out for him. Never doubted it. When he met Lela, he knew she was the one. He still believed that, but it broke his heart doing so. Because he also believed people had free will and could choose their paths contrary to what God desired for them. It looked like Lela was headed determinedly down that path, without a backward glance.

He had instinctively driven here because as a child he'd believed his Papa was as close as a man could get to being like God. As he stepped out of the car and headed toward the porch, Henry realized he still believed that.

And if he had ever needed that kind of comfort, it was now.

He walked up the porch steps, and finding the screen door latched, tapped lightly on its frame. He peered into the house, squinting into the darkened hallway. "Papa?" He saw Papa's cat hurriedly trotting to the door, meowing in the rusty alto she called a voice. "Hey, Smokestack!" She stood on her hind legs and stretched her front paws, hooking her claws into the screen as though trying to push the door open. "I don't think you can let me in, girl. It's latched." She lowered her dark grey body to the floor, sat down and curled her tail neatly around herself. "Papa!" Henry hollered this time.

From the back he heard, "Keep your shirt on, I'm headin' that way." He watched his grandfather come from the back of the house. From the looks of his rumpled shirt and his hair standing up like a spikey-do, Henry deduced a nap had been interrupted. "Hey, son! You woke me and Smokestack up. I was readin' and the next thing I knew she was jumpin' off the bed." Asa reached the door and flipped the latch open. "Come on in."

As Henry stepped inside the house, Asa glanced into his face. He stopped dead still. "Lord, son, what's the matter with you? Has somebody passed?"

"No, I – it's Lela, Papa. She says she's through with me."

For an alarming moment, both men feared that Henry was about to burst into little boy sobs, but he managed to wrestle control, hanging on to a shred of dignity.

"Com on in here and sit down. Let me get a cold drink of water for us. I'll be right back." He hobbled quickly to the kitchen, and Henry sank into the old couch in the living room. The cat arched her back and rubbed her head against his legs as he gave her a half-hearted pat. He put his head in his hands and didn't move until Asa came back into the room.

"Tell me it." Asa handed Henry a glass of water. "Drink this while you do it."

Henry took a sip and stared into the frosty glass as though it was a crystal ball about to tell his future. That is, if he'd thought he even had a future anymore. "You know I've hardly spoken with her since she found out about the hysterectomy. Her parents kept saying she was very upset and just to give her time. She called and asked me to come down to the hospital today." His voice cracked a little. "All it took was one look at her face and I knew I was in trouble. She says she's not gonna marry me or anybody else because she can't have children. I tried to tell her, Papa, that two can be a family, and I love her because she's Lela, not because I thought she could give me children."

"Did she say she don't love you no more?"

"No, as a matter of fact, she said she did love me. I know she does, but how can she do this to us *if* she does?"

Asa sighed heavily. "I 'spect she thinks she's bein' right noble. She knows you want younguns and she don't want to deny you that privilege. She figgers you'll get over her and marry some filly that can give you babies."

"Ha. If Lela never speaks to me again, I think I'm done with women till I'm a hundred."

"So what's your plan?"

"I don't have one. I got as far as coming here to get sympathy from you. That about wraps up my plan."

Asa looked at him in amazement. "You been tellin' me this is the woman you love and want to spend your life with and you *don't have a plan?* What is wrong with you, boy?"

"Well, I don't know what to do! I'm pretty clueless when things are going well, much less when they tank. I've never been smart when it comes to girls, you know that. Remember Jana Harper?"

"Lord, don't remind me of that mess. All she wanted was a little kiss and you 'bout had a heart attack."

"If I'd been a day over seven, I probably *woulda* had one. But seriously, Papa, I'm no better at this now than I was then. Trust me. It's true."

"I hope you're at least smarter now when it comes to what the Lord wants of you."

"I was – am – convinced that God put Lela in my life to become my wife."

"There you go, then."

"I also believe that we are free to make our own choices about obeying God and it looks to me like Lela has made a choice."

"That's true. So, are you gonna just let her walk off and be disobedient?"

"Believe me, Papa I didn't walk off, I was run off." He shook his head. "I don't know what else to do."

"She's hurt and mad at her Creator. I'm guessin' she's believed God has always give her the desires of her heart and now that He took one away she's callin' Him an Indian giver."

Henry studied that thought for a moment. "Makes sense." He squirmed a bit uncomfortably. "But isn't that kinda what He's done?"

Asa snorted. "That's our Lord for you. He puts a desire in your heart and then, mean like, He snatches it away from you at the last minute. Mind, He waits till He's purty shore you'll be blindsided by it."

Henry blushed. "I didn't mean it that way. I know He loves us beyond all understanding and would never cause us harm. I know He has our best interest at heart and sees the big picture we can't see. But what do I do now to help Lela get back on track? She's let me know she's not praying right now and doesn't intend to."

Asa leaned forward in his chair. He stared intently into Henry's eyes, as though willing Henry to understand what he was going to say. "Let's look at what the desires of her heart are. Hopefully the Lord Jesus was and is the first true desire, whether she'll admit that right now or not. What are the others? A husband and children. She thought those prayers had been answered. Then before any marryin' or nestin' could take place, her whole world come tumblin' down around her. She thinks God has taken away one of the things she most desires. If He's done took away one, He is obviously liable to take away the other, right?" Asa nodded his head, as though agreeing with himself. Before Henry could agree too, Asa kept right on talking. "Plus, why drag you into this awful thing when you can go off and find a woman who can have those babies she knows you want?"

"But I'd rather have zero babies and one Lela than one somebody else and lots of babies."

"Lela either don't really believe that or is playin' that old game of 'if I can't have it my way, I won't have it no way'."

"So what does that leave me to do?"

"Well, son, I'd advise you to start prayin' and listen real hard. Ask the good Lord to show you how to get Lela to see that He don't take away desires that He's placed in us."

Henry stared at Asa blankly. "But she *can't* have children."

"God knows that, Henry, He ain't surprised by none of this. Fact is, His plan is perfect for you and Lela. Stop tryin' to figger it out. Trust Him and He'll tell you exactly what you need to know." He patted Henry on the knee. "God ain't stopped by anything. This news has been devestatin' to us, but it ain't no big deal to Him. You just commence to pray and He'll not let you down. I know that for shore."

Henry left his grandfather's house feeling no more certain about what to do than when he had arrived. But somehow, he felt a whole lot more confident that he would soon know *exactly* what to do.

Chapter Twenty

A light tapping on her bedroom door made Lela glance up from the form she was filling out. "Come in."

Emmie poked her head around the door. "Are you ready to ride?"

Lela smiled at her friend. "Just about. I was filling out this questionnaire the college sent me about fall quarter."

"It's good to hear you're making plans."

Lela arched an eyebrow. "Why wouldn't I be? I have to get an education so I can get a job and leave home someday. I better take care of myself since I can't expect my parents to take care of me forever."

Emmie looked uncomfortable at Lela's vehemence. "Well, sure, Lela. I just meant I'm glad you're feeling better." She finished lamely.

Lela set down her pen and stood up. As she scooted the desk chair under the table she turned to Emmie. "Let's go. The butcher awaits."

"Oh, Lela, he seems like a good doctor. He saved your life."

Lela looked irritated. "What there is left of it. Some days I just wish – oh, never mind. Let's go."

Emmie stepped closer to her friend. "You know, things can be a lot better if you'll let them. Henry is worried sick. He loves you so much and wants you back in his life so badly."

Lela stepped back. "If Henry is so great, why don't you give it a stab? I'm sure he'd love the company."

Emmie looked as though she'd been sucker punched. Then her eyes flashed with anger. She slapped her forehead with her hand. "Now, why didn't I think of that? One's just as good as the other, right? Isn't that what you told him? I don't have a boyfriend at the moment, so why not? Where's my cell phone?" She pretended to look wildly around the room. " I'll call Henry right now and tell him since Lela has lost what little mind she ever had, I'm taking her place, mm'k? He'll be fine with that, he probably won't even notice the difference." This time when she stepped closer to Lela it was with anger. "How dare you throw your whole future away because something, even something as big as this, has happened to you? You need to stop listening to your feelings and start listening to God. He's trying to tell you something!" With that she stormed out the bedroom door.

"Wait!" Lela called, looking for her purse. "You can't leave me! I'm not allowed to drive yet!"

"Then explain to me how you're managing to drive everyone completely crazy!" Emmie hollered from the hall. She turned back toward the bedroom as Lela hurried out the door. "Your parents are sick with worry. Henry is like a ghost. He's hardly eating, he's not working even though they're hounding him about the Christmas CD and his parents are almost as worried as yours are. You, Lela Sawyer, should be ashamed of yourself."

Lela dropped her head. "I am, Emmie. But it doesn't change anything. I simply can't do this to Henry." She looked up at her friend, tears pooled in her eyes. "Everyone thinks I'm doing this because I'm selfish, or feeling sorry for myself. But I'm doing it because Henry deserves better. He *needs* to be a daddy. He needs a wife who can complete him and give him more joy than pain. I'm not up to the job." She began to cry. "I know I should be turning to God, but I can't find Him right now. I know I should be grateful that the doctor saved my life, but I'm not. I wish I never had to get up out of bed again."

"Oh, Lela, honey, come here." Emmie wrapped her arms around her. "I'm so sorry. But you're still dead wrong. We all know it. But I guess it doesn't matter how much we know. It's you who's got to live your life." She patted Lela's back. "Come on, you're going to be late for your appointment and your mother will kill us both."

At the doctor's, the waiting room was full of pregnant women and mothers with new babies. Lela kept her head buried in a magazine. Emmie kept looking around the room, then at the top of her friend's head. She finally dug into her purse and got a tissue to stem the sniffles.

When they called Lela back, Emmie got up too, but Lela motioned her to sit back down and went toward the examining room alone.

She was sitting in her paper gown, swinging her feet back and forth when the doctor came in. He smiled at her and asked, "How are you doing?"

"Okay, I guess."

"Well, let's check and see." The nurse came in to stand by and watch the doctor perform his examination. After poking and prodding and asking more than once, "Does that hurt?" He finished up. "You can sit up now – careful – roll over to your side first. You're pretty much healed, but we don't want to strain those muscles just yet." He glanced at the nurse. "Thanks, we're finished with the physical exam. You can leave."

The nurse rushed out as the doctor flipped open Lela's chart to study. He glanced at the computer monitor and typed a few notes. When he finished, he leaned up against the counter, crossed his arms over his chest and looked at Lela. "It's been six weeks since surgery. You appear to be doing great physically. I gather no hot flashes or other symptoms of early onset menopause?"

"No. I've not had any symptoms."

"That's a relief. I had hoped I'd left enough of that ovary to prevent it and it looks like I did." He cocked his head toward her. "However; you look like you've lost your best friend. How are you dealing with all this?"

She shrugged her shoulders. "Trying to get by, I guess. I'm still planning on going to school this fall."

"That's good. And now you'll have more freedom to get out because I'm releasing you to start driving. How about that young man of yours? He looked like a good catch." The doctor grinned at her.

Lela's eyes narrowed dangerously. "You know, if one more person asks me about Henry, I'm going to explode. Just because he's a famous rock star is no reason to think he's a good catch."

The doctor looked at her blankly. "That tall skinny blond guy that hung around the hospital hovering over you nonstop is a *rock star*?" He sounded as if he did not believe Lela for one second.

"Yes he is." She said irritably.

"Ah. Well, that explains the goofy hair, anyway." He shook his head. "Rock star notwithstanding, he is crazy about you. Don't tell me you're playing the martyr over this hysterectomy and have set him free?"

If Lela could have jumped off the table and marched off in a huff, she would have. However; the paper gown that was minus a back precluded that maneuver. "You can call it what you want to, not that it's any of your business, but I'm not seeing him anymore."

"I thought you were way smarter than that."

Lela looked up at him defiantly, tears brightening her eyes. "You have no idea what I've been through. If anybody should understand I can't have children, it should be you. After all, you're the one who took everything out." She ended bitterly.

"Ouch. If I wasn't so thick skinned that would hurt my feelings. I happen to know it saved your life, though. You're not the only person this has ever happened to." He stopped for a moment, as though considering what he was about to say. "Look, Lela, it just so happens I do kind of know what you're going through. My wife had an emergency hysterectomy shortly after we were married due to injuries from a near fatal car wreck. She went through hell afterwards. She wasn't quite as fortunate as you, because she was suddenly in full-blown menopause at age twenty-three. She begged me to divorce her so I could marry somebody who could give me children. Pffft. Women are crazy, I tell ya. I'd just been scared out of my mind that I was going to lose her, and here she was asking me for a divorce over the fact she couldn't get pregnant. If she had gone out of my life, I would have lost my mind. Not having children wasn't as bad – how could I miss something I'd never had? But to lose her? Missing her would have been unbearable."

"Is she healthy now?"

"Yep, and lives a full life. She's a professional woman, does volunteer work with disabled kids and spoils me to no end."

Lela smiled slightly. "I'm glad she's all right."

"Me too." He stood straighter. "I don't need to see you for three months. If you can't shake this sadness, please see a counselor. This isn't something easy to come to terms with. I gave your mother several names of excellent therapists before you were discharged from the hospital. Do yourself a favor and visit one." He started out the door. "And really, really think about giving Mr. Rock Star a second chance, okay?"

Lela nodded. "Thanks."

He closed the door behind him. Lela sighed, scooted carefully off the examining table and gathered her clothes up. She wearily wondered when everyone would just leave her alone.

Chapter
Twenty-One

*H*enry paced. He prayed. He talked with Pastor James, his parents, Lela's parents, his friends and Lela's friends. He would have talked to rank strangers if he had believed it would have done any good.

He lost sleep, he lost weight, he thought he might lose his mind. But he never lost his faith.

He called his agent and instructed him to begin contacting musicians and set up studio time for recording. Regardless of how the upcoming weekend turned out, he had legal and professional obligations to fulfill, and time had run out for putting them off any longer.

He stood before the congregation of his church and talked with them about what was on his heart. He asked them to pray specifically for God's will and direction in this endeavor. They agreed with him in prayer.

Henry had prepared lessons. He had prepared concerts. But he felt like he had never prepared for anything more important than this.

Because this could be the single most important thing for which he had ever prepared.

Henry pulled up to Lela's house, his heart going like a trip hammer. If this didn't work, he knew there was nothing left for him to try. His friends got out of the back seat, and they all headed to the door.

As planned, Lela's parents had made themselves unavailable to answer the knock, so after some time, Lela finally opened the front door. She gazed dully at Henry, at first not realizing anyone stood behind him. He spoke and moved aside, introducing his companions. "Lela, these are my dear friends, Jack and Jordie Worley."

Jack was holding the hand of a small boy, while Jordie held a new baby in her arms. "This is their son, Samuel," Henry said, as he pointed to the toddler. "And this little bundle is Meredith."

Lela was stunned. *How could Henry do this to her?* She looked beyond Henry to the couple, trying to control her emotions. "Please, come in." She reached up to her tousled hair, "I'm sorry for the way I look, I didn't expect company."

"Don't worry, you look fine." Henry said, ushering them all in as Lela's mother entered the foyer.

"Come in, come in." Vicki smiled warmly at them. "Oh, what a beautiful baby! And who is this?" She asked looking down at the little boy.

"I'm Samuel. Who are you?"

"I'm Lela's mother." She smiled. "Please, come on into the living room and have a seat."

The Worleys followed Lela's mother. Henry and Lela lagged behind. As soon as they were out of earshot, Lela hissed at Henry, "How could you do this to me? How could you bring a baby into this house now?"

Henry pushed his face within an inch of hers, and this time he was the one squinting. Rapid fire, he whispered back, "They wanted to see you! When we didn't know if you were going to make it after surgery, and all the days that followed, they took turns, Lela, twenty-four hours a day, praying for you non-stop. That means they were up in the middle of the night. They interrupted their workdays. They never failed you in prayer. How could I not invite them to meet you when they asked, now that you're healing?"

Taken aback by his fervor, Lela nodded. "I guess you're right. It's just so hard." Her voice quivered and she swayed slightly. Henry reached out to steady her, but she put her hand up to stop him. "Don't, Henry. Please don't. I'm fine." Then her eyes narrowed suspiciously. "Did you not tell them we broke up?"

Before he could answer, Lela's mother came into the foyer. "Lela? Henry? I've offered your friends refreshment." She handed Lela a glass of tea. "Henry, would you like a Coke or tea?"

"Coke's fine, thanks. We're coming." They turned, walking into the living room. The Worleys were seated on the couch. Lela took the big armchair, propping pillows protectively around herself. Henry sat in the rocker. Lela's mother went into the kitchen.

"Henry tells me you prayed for me a lot. Thank you. I appreciate it." Her voice was stilted and formal.

"You are so welcome. That's what brothers and sisters in Christ do." Jordie replied.

Samuel disengaged himself from his father's arms and looked up at his mother. "She cry. Why that girl sad?"

Jordie smiled apologetically toward Lela. "Samuel is only three, he says what's on his mind." She looked down at him. "Miss Lela was really sick and the doctors had to help her a lot. She's still not completely well, and maybe her tummy is sore from where the doctors helped her."

Samuel walked over to Lela and put one slightly grubby hand on her knee. "I sorry. Jesus will help. He helps me when I get a booboo."

Lela smiled weakly at him. "I know. Thank you for telling me, though." She glanced at Henry. "Will you all please excuse me just a minute?" She got up slowly and walked into the kitchen, her back stiff, her body shaking.

Jack looked at his friend. "Henry, maybe this wasn't such a good idea. I mean, you're killing her here."

"You're aware of how I've prayed and prayed about this. I *know* it's the right thing. She won't talk to me. This is the only thing that might keep me from losing her. I *can't* lose her, Jack. I just can't." Henry closed his eyes trying to compose himself.

They were silent until Lela and her mother came back into the room. Vicki handed out the drinks, then perched herself on the edge of a chair. Hands clasped tightly together, she cast a sideways glance at Lela.

Kathi Harper Hill

Henry took a shaky swig of his Coke and stood. He walked over to Jordie and took the baby in his arms. Lela watched him. She looked up at Henry, and in a trembling voice said, "You look like a natural. You'll be a great daddy someday."

"I'm counting on it." He shifted the baby a little, walking toward Lela. "Why don't you hold Meredith for a minute?"

"Oh, no, Henry, please-"

"It's okay. We'll prop you up so you don't bear the weight, it won't hurt you."

To the contrary, Lela looked up with more raw pain in her eyes than Henry had ever seen in anyone. He blinked rapidly and stiffened his resolve as he handed the infant to her. Lela looked down at the baby, who wiggled a little, pursed her lips, then settled back into sleep. "She's beautiful." Lela looked at the tiny eyelashes, the button nose, the little hands that were curled into themselves. She thought she might just fall apart and never be able to pull herself back together again. One lone tear streaked down her cheek, and landed with a soft plop on the baby's blanket.

Henry looked at Jordie. "How old was Meredith when you got her?"

Lela's head jerked up. "Got her? What do you mean, *got* her?"

Jordie stood and went to Lela. Dropping to her knees, she grasped Lela's hand. "When I was fifteen years old I got a rare form of cancer. The treatment saved my life. But it also made me sterile." She tilted her head looking back in memory. "I remember lying in the hospital bed; feeling like my world had just ended. I grieved over the children I would never have. And I grieved for the mother I would never be." She reached out and stroked Meredith's tiny hand. The baby grasped her mother's finger in reflex. "From then on out, I avoided any relationship with boys." Jordie nodded toward her husband. "Then Mr. I Won't Take No For An Answer showed up." Jack grinned at his wife. "I turned him away, over and over. Finally one day I lit into him. I told him he didn't really know me, because if he did, he wouldn't want me. That I wasn't a whole person. He eyed me up and down and said I looked pretty whole to him. Boy, that made me mad! I got in his face and I let him know right quick I wasn't even a real woman, and thanks to all I'd been through, I could never be a mother. And you know what he

150

did? He laughed! Then he just shook his head. He asked me: '*Jordie, do you want to be pregnant, or do you want to be a mother?*' I looked at him like he was crazy." Jordie squeezed Lela's hand. "He saw the solution as a simple thing. Because, you see, Jack is adopted. I had been so wrapped up in my grief and pain and anger, I couldn't see outside my bitter little box. What Jack said to me changed my whole world. I suddenly realized I *could* have what I had longed to have. And I do. Samuel and Meredith are the most wonderful gifts. Lela, I love them so much. We are blessed beyond measure."

Lela looked down at the sleeping baby. "What's not to love?" She touched Meredith's face, which made the baby frown. As Lela's finger traced her lips, Meredith began to suck and then grunted when nothing was forthcoming. She opened her eyes and looked accusingly at Lela, puckered up and started wailing. The adults laughed as Lela said, "Take your child and feed her. I think I've awakened the beast within."

Jordie scooped up the baby as Jack quickly handed her a bottle.

Lela looked at Henry. "You planned this very well."

"Yeah."

"Thank you, Henry." Lela smiled at them. "Thank you all so much."

Chapter Twenty-Two

enry and Lela sat in the den. The Worleys had driven off in Henry's car, with Art promising to get Henry home.

The silence was deafening. After all the noise of the baby crying, Samuel warming up to everyone and showing off his Indian war whoop, and adults chatting with giddy relief over Lela's reaction, the awkward quiet seemed even more profound.

Vicki and Art had mysteriously disappeared to parts unknown, so they were alone with one another.

Totally alone.

Henry cleared his throat. "So, uh, Jordie and Jack are nice people, huh?"

"Very nice."

"They've got great kids, haven't they?"

"Great kids."

"The adoption agency they used was founded by a church." Henry felt like he was on the verge of babbling. "The agency makes sure all the birth parents have an opportunity to know Christ. They only consider mature Christian couples when choosing adoptive parents."

"Really?"

"Yeah, really."

"I guess we've got some growing up to do then."

Kathi Harper Hill

Henry's eyes lit with hope. "Are you saying you'd be willing to adopt children?"

"That's what I'm saying."

"Does that mean you're going to marry me after all?"

"Duh, Henry."

Henry practiced one of Samuel's Indian war whoops.

Lela clapped her hands over her ears. "Henry, for Heaven's sake! What was that for?"

"I'm so relieved! I've been so worried! Now I can tell him everything is going to be all right."

"Tell *who* everything is going to be all right?" She asked, puzzled.

"Pistol. Who else? Why, just the other night he was whining as only a dog can do, saying '*Rhere's Rera? Rot roe, Henwry*.'"

"Pistol's not Scooby Doo, Henry."

"He's part Scooby. The Great Dane part."

"Uh-huh." She sighed. "Did I mention there's a *lot* of growing up to do? Henry, could you scoot over here just a little closer?"

"Sure." He slid over. In his very best Scooby voice he asked, "Rike ris?"

Lela kissed him soundly on the mouth.

Anything to shut him up.

Chapter Twenty-Three

*J*une twentieth finally arrived. The church was packed. The front was decorated with cascading roses in the palest of pink down to the deepest of pink, bringing out the rich jewel tones of the stained glass windows. Greenery covered every other inch.

Henry stood with his father just beyond the double doors to the side of the pulpit. He could hear music playing softly as people chattered as though they didn't have a care in the world. He tugged at the tight collar of his shirt, wishing he could loosen the bow tie just a little bit, as it was clearly cutting off his life force. He glanced down at the rose in his lapel, making sure it hadn't turned upside down or something. He turned to his father. "Did you remember the ring?"

His father sighed heavily. "For at least the sixth time, yes indeed, I have the ring." He patted his coat pocket. "Right here. Safe and sound. But if we see him before the wedding begins, do *not* mention it to Samuel, because he thinks the little plastic ring pinned onto the pillow is the real deal."

"Don't worry. He's already told me all about it. He also shared the promise to his mama that he wouldn't do the Indian war whoop until after the reception."

Henry felt a hand on his shoulder and he turned to see Pastor James smiling at him. "Nervous?"

"Lord, that's the truth. I may faint. Is there any record of grooms faintin'?"

"I wouldn't be a bit surprised." Pastor James looked him over. "You look handsome."

"I look like a penguin in a fright wig. But I know for a fact the bride loves me regardless."

Art, Asa, and Henry's buddies appeared, as did Lela's pastor, who would be performing the ceremony. The pastor shook hands all around, then gathered Henry in a bear hug, semi-squashing the rose. "Let's have a word of prayer and get this show on the road."

Asa beamed at Henry as the men formed a circle and bowed their heads.

Henry prayed he wouldn't really faint.

Lela stood looking at herself in the mirror. Her hair was piled loosely on top of her head, tendrils escaping here and there. She had picked the laciest, most Victorian wedding gown she could find, fingering it every time she passed by her closet. Now she turned left and right, admiring how it fit her like a glove. The antique diamond-encrusted sapphire sat nestled in the hollow of her neck, the tiny chain almost invisible. The earrings, peaking through the cinnamon curls slipping free, were tiny twins to the necklace. She grinned. She looked at *least* twenty-five all dolled up like this, and she was going to be sure and point that out to Henry as soon as the wedding ceremony was over.

Her mother walked up behind her. "You are a vision, Lela." Tears began to pool in her eyes. "I will *not* cry! I can't mess up my face. I spent way too much money on it."

Lela smiled at her mother as she turned toward her. "How is Emmie holding up?"

Her mother rolled her eyes. "Don't ask, honey, don't ask. We're making her drink sips of Sprite, so she'll probably have to pee any minute."

They snickered together as they opened the door and stepped into the foyer where the semi-hysterical Emmie stood with the other three bridesmaids. Lela glanced down at Emmie's little five-year-old cousin, Polly, who had excitedly agreed to be the flower girl. Her basket was full of pink rose petals and the foyer smelled sweetly of them. She agreed with solemn maturity to make sure four-year-old Samuel stayed in step. He stood next to her, holding her hand.

The door eased open and Henry's mother slipped in. She clasped her hands under her chin. "You are beautiful! What a lucky man my son is."

"Thanks." Lela hugged her.

Jean Smithfield bustled in. She had taken on the task as wedding coordinator, and by the look on her face, took it as serious business. "Okay, ladies, it's almost time."

Both mothers gave another quick hug to Lela as she and the bridesmaids moved themselves with the children into the side room.

Suddenly Henry stood alone with his father. He felt rooted to the spot. Although he'd promised not to, his hand crept upward to paw through his hair. Just in the nick of time, his daddy nudged him and whispered, "Let's go, son."

They walked out to the front of the altar. Henry, as though in a dream, watched as one of his buddies escorted his mother in. Then another buddy seated Vicki.

The music changed slightly, and the back doors opened. The groomsmen and bridesmaids walked slowly toward the front of the church.

Henry started sweating.

Then Samuel and Polly came out, stopping between each step. Polly carefully strew rose petals, One. Petal. At. A. Time., down the isle. As they triumphantly reached the front, Samuel waved wildly to the congregation.

Henry feared Samuel would change his mind about the Indian war whoop.

Henry almost jumped out of his skin when the organ trumpeted loudly, announcing the dramatic re-opening of the double doors.

The congregation rose as one, turning to watch with eager anticipation.

Lela stepped out, her hand lightly resting on her father's arm. Tears blurred Henry's vision for a moment. She was the most beautiful creature he had ever seen.

She gazed at his face, and he could see tears glistening in her eyes, too.

As Henry watched Lela walk steadily toward him, he believed his heart would surely burst with thanksgiving for this moment.

Lela and her father stopped at the altar. Pastor James stepped forward and led them in the opening prayer.

Lela's pastor read Scripture. Turning, he asked, "Who gives this bride away?"

"Her mother and I." Stepping back, her father gently placed Lela's hand on Henry's arm.

Henry, gazing into Lela's eyes, placed his hand on top of hers.

It felt as though time stood still.

The pianist hit a note for the third time and Henry was brought out of his hypnotic state by congregational tittering.

He blinked slowly, blushing with embarrassment. Lela smiled at him reassuringly and squeezed his hand.

Taking a deep breath, Henry sang to his bride.

Then, just like that, it was over.

Lela's pastor smiled benevolently upon the couple as Henry kissed his bride. Then, turning them to face the congregation, he announced: "Ladies and gentlemen, I present to you for the very first time, Mr. and Mrs. Henry Fields!"

For a moment in time, they looked out at all the smiling faces. They saw the people who had prayed for them diligently through the bad and good. They saw the people who would *always* love them and pray for them and hold them accountable. They saw the people who would be the weave in the tapestry of their lives as husband and wife. Their hearts swelled with gratitude for the gift of these people.

Then they took off toward the rest of their lives, almost running down the aisle to the accompaniment of merry music and wild applause.

It was the best standing ovation Henry Fields had ever received.

Epilogue

Three years later:

The social worker walked into the waiting area holding a tiny bundle wrapped in blue.

Henry nodded to Lela and she stepped forward, eagerly reaching out her arms. Mrs. Worth gently transferred the baby to Lela and slipped the blanket from his tiny head as she moved away.

Lela gasped. Henry shook his head in mock dismay. "Adoption as an excuse won't hold water. He is definitely gonna blame <u>you</u> for these." Henry brushed one finger across the flaming red curls that covered the baby's head.

At Henry's touch, the baby frowned and opened his eyes. He stared up at Henry with deep pools of dark navy. "Well, hello there Sawyer Leland Fields. Welcome to the world. What do you think about us?"

The baby shut his eyes and then gave a mighty yawn, his tiny hands balled up in fists on each side of his head as he relaxed back into sleep. "I see he's going to bore easily like his daddy." Lela teased.

"I don't bore easily, I just get distracted."

"You want a turn?"

"Oh, yeah. Come here, buddy." Henry gingerly scooped the baby up into his arms and kissed the top of the tiny head. "Oh, man, Lela, this is our baby! Our son!"

Mrs. Worth smiled at them both. "Let's have prayer over this little one before you leave." She placed a hand on each of their shoulders, forming a circle of warmth around the newborn. "Great and Mighty God, we come before You to praise and worship at Your Throne of Mercy. With humble heart I give thanks for the parents You have chosen for this male child. May he be taught to have Your love in his heart, Your Name upon his lips and the desire inside his spirit to serve You all his days, becoming Your Will and Your Nature. Give these new parents strength and wisdom to grow this child up in a way that will be pleasing to You. May he joyfully fulfill the destiny You place before him and may he do it with a willingness that will humble those who observe him. We commit Sawyer Leland Fields into Your Beautiful and Graceful Hands, for You, Father, hold all of us in Your Palm. For this, we are ever thankful, Lord. Go now in peace family, and fulfill God's great destiny. In the name of the Son of the Living God, Jesus Christ, we offer up this petition. Amen and Amen."

And with that beautiful, bountiful blessing, the Field's family journeyed home.

LaVergne, TN USA
04 November 2009
163071LV00004B/13/P